P9-EMO-340

DRAGONS VS. UNICORNS

DRAGONS VS. UNICORNS

DR. KATE BIBERDORF
WITH HILLARY HOMZIE

Philomel Books

morning

Hi! My Name is Dr. Kate Biberdorf, but most people call me Kate the Chemist. I perform explosive science experiments on national TV when I'm not in Austin, Texas, teaching chemistry classes. Besides being the best science in the entire world, chemistry is the study of energy and matter, and their interactions with each other. Like how I can use cornstarch to breathe fire or liquid nitrogen to freeze Cheetos! If you read *Dragons vs. Unicorns* carefully, you will see how Little Kate the Chemist uses chemistry to solve problems in her everyday life.

But remember, none of the experiments in this book should be done without the supervision of a trained professional! If you are looking for some fun, safe, at-home experiments, check out my companion book, *Kate the Chemist: The Big Book of Experiments*. (I've included one experiment from that book in the back of this one—how to make unicorn glue!)

And one more thing: Science is all about making predictions (or forming hypotheses), which you can do right now! Who do you think will win? The dragons or the unicorns? Let's find out—it's time for Kate the Chemist's first adventure.

XOXO,

Kate

PHILOMEL BOOKS
An imprint of Penguin Random House LLC, New York

First published in the United States of America by Philomel, an imprint of Penguin Random House LLC, 2020.

Visit us online at penguinrandomhouse.com

Library of Congress Cataloging-in-Publication Data is available.

Printed in the United States of America

ISBN 9780593116555

1 3 5 7 9 10 8 6 4 2

Edited by Jill Santopolo. Designed by Lori Thorn.
Text set in ITC Stone Serif.

To my dragons (Chelsea, Caitlin, Amanda)

and my unicorns (Katie, Becky, Brittany).

This is for you.

TABLE OF CONTENTS

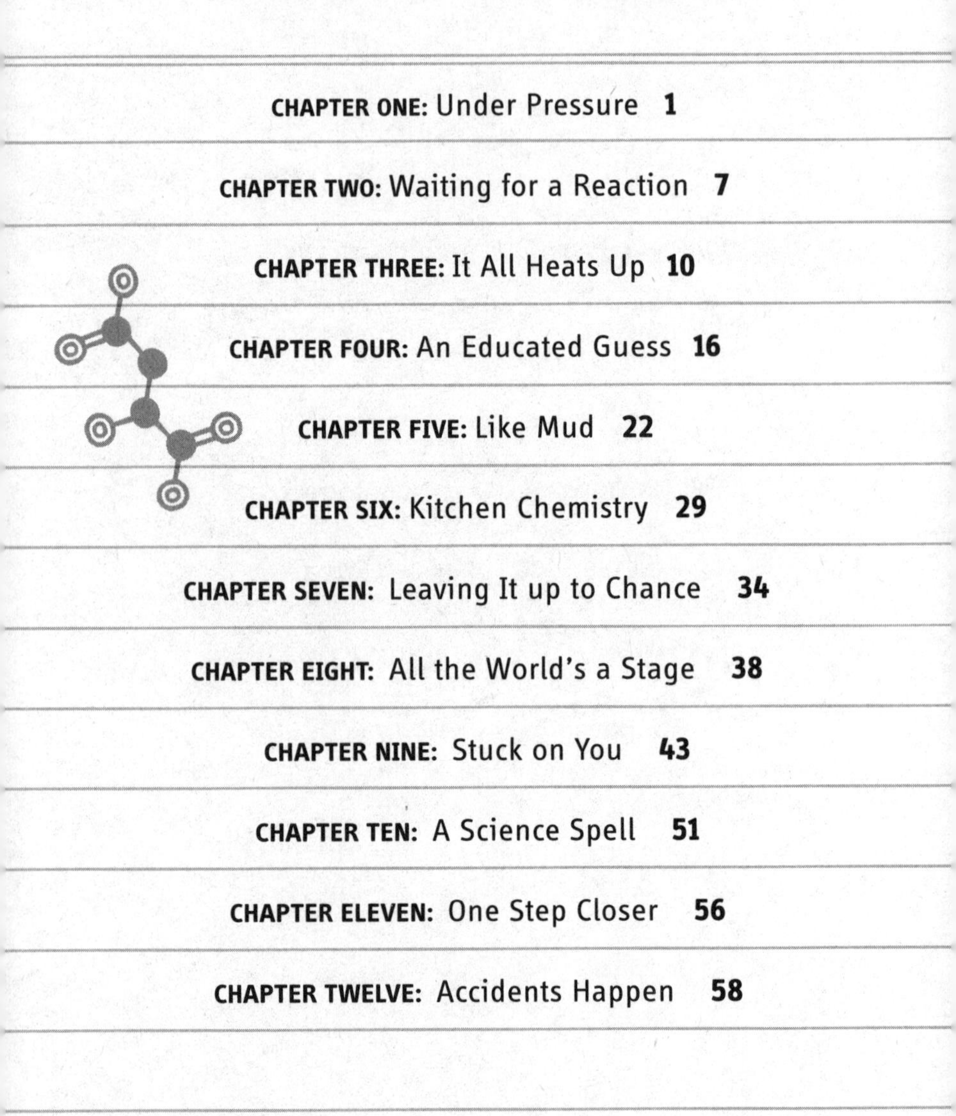

CHAPTER ONE

UNDER PRESSURE

Pressure (noun). When molecules work together to apply a force. Like if kindergartners push over an ice-cream truck at recess, or when lava forces its way out of a volcano.

BREATHING FIRE IS EASY.

At least that was what I told myself. I stood in the science lab after school in front of a couple dozen fourth and fifth graders. All waiting on me. No pressure.

"Ready, Kate?" asked Ms. Daly, our after-school chemistry club advisor.

"I was born ready!" I pumped my arm in the air like I was in the huddle before a soccer game.

"Egg-cellent," said Ms. Daly. It was her typical cornball humor. Mostly because of

this stinky experiment we did last April that turned raw eggs into bouncy balls. A bunch rolled all over the place, and one got lost in the radiator.

Only there weren't rotten bouncy eggs involved in my demo.

Instead:

1 blowtorch (with a steady base so the school wouldn't catch on fire)
1 big mouth (mine—words pretty much launched out of it and thoughts came later)
2 scoops of cornstarch (nothing to do with Ms. Daly's cornball humor. It had to do with carbon.)
1 straw (reusable, my BFF Birdie made sure of it)
2 legs (to run with if things got too explosive)
1 bucket (to spit out the cornstarch)
2 best friends (1 to hold the fire extinguisher and 1 to cheer me on)
1 glass of water (to rinse out my mouth after the demo)
1 big bowl of water (safety, duh!)
1 fire blanket (Unlike Supergirl, the girl of steel, I'm fully human.)

Ms. Daly secured the blowtorch onto a nearby desk. With its attachable base, it looked like a missile.

"It's ready," she declared. Soon a 2,000-degree flame would spew out of its brass nozzle. Not just anywhere. A foot from my head.

I swallowed hard. Why did I volunteer for this again?

Chairs scraped the floor. Kids leaned forward to see better.

Normally, we got about a dozen for our Friday meetings.

Today, three dozen crammed into the room.

It was the very last meeting before fall break, and everyone had flocked here to see me. I didn't want to blow it.

Strike that. I NEEDED to blow it—cornstarch, I mean, spitting straight toward the flame to make a gigantic sizzling fireball.

"Is that a real torch?" asked Avery Cooper, a chemistry club regular who played midfield on my soccer team. She pointed so enthusiastically that her short blonde braids bobbed. "It looks like a prop from my dads' theater."

"Oh, it's real all right," I said.

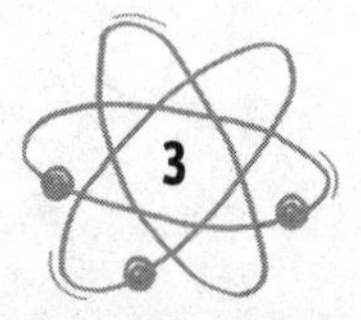

"I'll vouch for that," said Ms. Daly. She should know. She's a retired air force flight engineer. She knocked on the tank with a wrench from her tool belt. The silver wrench was the same color as her cap of short hair. "It's loaded with fuel," she said.

"Awesome," sniffed a nasally fourth grader in an Avengers T-shirt. He made a *kaboom* sound that was a little too phlegmy.

"It's going to be a beautiful swirl of color," said Birdie Bhatt in a hushed voice. Of course Birdie would say that. She's my best friend and really amazing at drawing, especially unicorns.

"Take a step back," instructed Ms. Daly, shooing everyone with her arms. "You should be in the second row. Just in case."

"In case of what?" snapped Phoenix Altman, who locked eyes with Avery.

"It's only a precaution," said Ms. Daly. Just like the fire blanket. And the fire extinguisher that Elijah Williams, my other best friend and also my next-door neighbor, was holding.

For a moment, regret zipped inside me like hot gas

molecules. Had I really declared in a not-so-quiet voice during recess that I could breathe fire?

Yup. Speak-and-then-think Kate Crawford at your service!

If I had known what was going to happen afterward, would I have breathed fire?

That's complicated.

Because it wasn't just the fire breathing demo.

It was all the stuff days later. Because of the demo. Because of me.

But I didn't know any of that then. I just knew I had to breathe fire like Dr. Caroline, on YouTube. It's not only because she blows things up and makes the best and weirdest messes. Or because of her hot-pink lab coat and cool shoes. It's because by listening to her, I realized that chemistry is way more than a bunch of facts in a book. Chemistry is what you eat, it's how you sleep, it's why shampoo stings your eyes in the shower. You can taste science, you can smell it. And you can watch it explode. And that was the reason I had to breathe fire.

It was also why weird things

started happening to me. You might call them messages. Or formulas that didn't make sense.

And when something doesn't make sense, I, Kate Crawford, get very, very curious and just have to figure it out.

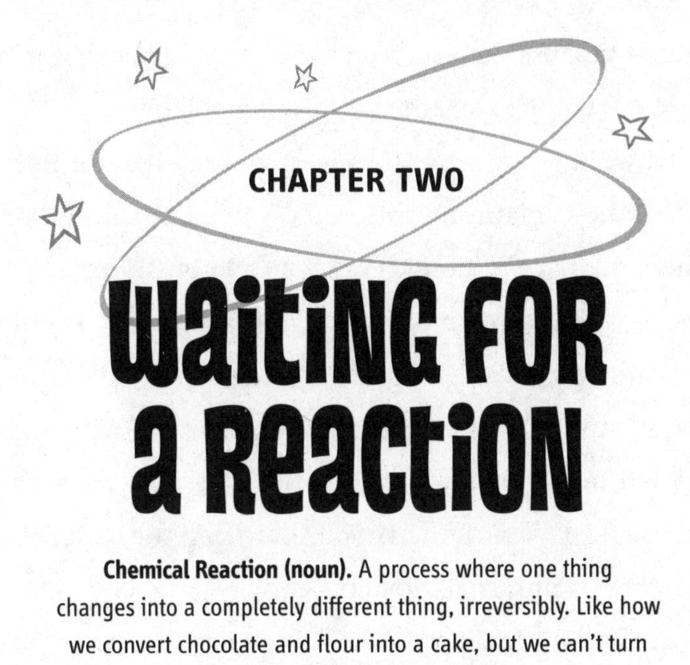

CHAPTER TWO

WAITING FOR A REACTION

Chemical Reaction (noun). A process where one thing changes into a completely different thing, irreversibly. Like how we convert chocolate and flour into a cake, but we can't turn a cake into chocolate and flour!

ELIJAH LIFTED THE FIRE EXTINGUISHER over his short afro, grunting as if it were heavy, which it wasn't. He could be such a drama king. "I'm on it," he said. "Just call me the Firefighter."

Birdie whipped out her phone. Well, not her phone. Her older sister Meela's. Birdie had dropped hers in the pond by my house.

Mostly because she had been a little shocked when I told her I was going to breathe fire after school today.

I wasn't sure why she was surprised. It's not like I hadn't been planning this demo since last spring. Ms. Daly said that if I wrote an essay on combustion (the science word for fire) and showed her I was ready, I could breathe fire when I got to fifth grade. So I had written about my need to understand fire, starting with why toasted marshmallows taste better (the heat from the fire breaks a whole bunch of bonds within the molecules creating yummy marshmallow goo).

Ms. Daly loved it. And now, guess what? It was October 2, and I had been a fifth grader for thirty days. And don't say *not that anyone was counting*. Because I was. I love math.

Ms. Daly handed me a pale blue fire-resistant lab coat. "More safety precautions," she said firmly.

My hair was already pulled back into a ponytail. And the bowl of water sat on a nearby counter. I rolled up the sleeves of the lab coat. Even though I was tall for

ten, the long coat brushed the tips of my cowboy boots. The coat would help keep me safe because it was made from a fabric that was not supposed to melt and would protect me from heat. It was okay that it smelled bad and made me look like I was wearing ugly pajamas that my grandma Dort wouldn't wear, even if you paid her.

I crossed my fingers and toes that everything would go exactly as I had practiced.

CHAPTER THREE

IT ALL HEATS UP

Exothermic Reaction (noun). It's as if the molecules are on the monkey bars, and they can't hang out for a long time, so they drop down to the sand and chill. When they move, heat is released.

I GRABBED THE CUP FILLED with cornstarch and tossed it back into my mouth.

The saliva was sucked from inside my cheeks. Cornstarch absorbs moisture. It's the first weird part of breathing fire.

I had practiced nine times. With Ms. Daly in the room, of course. Since the first Friday after school started, we had carefully gone over each and every step of the demo. And I had also practiced spitting the cornstarch with a fake blowtorch at home all summer.

Ms. Daly grabbed the propane torch to double-check its position.

Lots of "whoas" and lots of "she's not serious" flew through the room.

I wanted to yell, "You bet!" But then I would swallow cornstarch, and that wouldn't be fun.

Because I could choke. Or maybe get sick.

Ms. Daly clicked the torch to ignite the fire. With a loud hiss, the blowtorch blasted a jet of gas right next to my face.

Holy jeans! This was fire.

Okay, now I was shaking in my special birthday cowboy boots. Still, I had dreamed about this moment for so long.

I snatched the reusable teal straw.

This was the hardest part. I had to blow the cornstarch in my mouth through the straw toward the flame. It was like having a mouth full of peas and a pea shooter. It was harder though, because my mouth felt like cotton.

Most fire blowers don't use straws. But Ms. Daly had decided a foot-long one would keep my head a safe distance from the blowtorch. Out of the corner of my eye, I spied my mom and little brother, Liam, peeking in from

the back window. Everyone knew Liam was my brother because we had the exact same hair color. Light brown with bright gold highlights. Only mine was super long, and his was super short. And everyone recognized my mother. Especially since she just happened to be the principal of Rosalind Franklin Elementary. But I knew she didn't want to distract me.

It made me feel better seeing her. But also a tiny bit more nervous, too.

"Don't step past this line." Ms. Daly pointed to the red duct tape on the floor, which she'd put there so I wouldn't get too close to the flames.

Lunging forward, I stopped in front of the red line. From my gut—with everything I had—I blew out the cornstarch through the straw. Like after the ref blew a whistle at the start of a soccer game, I was in the zone.

A giant fireball whooshed out of the straw. It was a serious blast. Longer and bigger and brighter than in any practice run.

I heard gasps of disbelief and awe.

The red-hot ball of sizzling fuel punched out like a fist.

Oh no! It was

going to incinerate Ms. Daly's cactus on the windowsill.

Kids screamed, "Fire!"

The cactus's needles started to singe.

"It's going to explode!" Avery shouted. She raced to the front of the room, grabbed the bowl of water, and tossed it on the burning cactus. Only it missed the cactus and drenched me instead.

Elijah pulled out the pin on the fire extinguisher and pushed down on the trigger. A spray of foam whooshed out of the tank. Sweeping back and forth, he blasted out the flames. Soon white extinguisher goop covered the cactus.

It was saved! Water dripped down my chin, but I didn't mind.

Everyone clapped wildly, and I high-fived Elijah, who was grinning from ear to ear. "Thank you," I wanted to say, but yucky cornstarch clogged my mouth.

Immediately, I spat out the cornstarch into the bucket and took a big swig of water. You definitely didn't want to eat that stuff.

Trust me, it was chalky not tasty.

"Do it again!" kids shouted. They meant breathe fire, not spew cornstarch.

“But don’t burn any plants,” said Avery.

“Good plan,” said Ms. Daly. “But it’s a prickly pear. Hopefully, it will resprout.”

“It looked like fire spit right out of her mouth,” said someone in the very back.

My heart pounded louder than Elijah’s drums in his garage. I did it. Oh yeah! I gave Elijah another high five. I gave Ms. Daly a high five just as Mom and Liam rushed into the science lab.

“I’m so happy the fire is out,” said Mom in her principal voice.

“That was cool,” exclaimed Liam. I bounced up and down like the cement floor was a trampoline. I was so happy, I could spring to the ceiling.

I happily and drippily bounced through some of Ms. Daly’s explanations. Like how cornstarch was the fuel. And that it worked really well because it had carbon in it. The more carbon, the bigger the fire.

It had definitely been a big wow!

A fourth grader in a basketball shirt raised his hand. “I want to breathe fire.”

And then a fifth grader with a shiny ponytail that spurted out of the top of her head yelled, “Me too!” Her

name was Julia Yoon, and she was president of the student council. She liked to be in charge, just like me. "Can we try it now?" she asked. "Please?"

Ms. Daly smiled tightly. "Not right now," she said. And I could hear Avery whispering, "So unfair." The basketball shirt kid rolled his eyes.

"Kate worked hard to understand how fire breathing worked," continued Ms. Daly, "and practiced a lot. With adult supervision. However, I'd love for you all to start thinking about your own science projects. You could enter them in our upcoming science fair."

Then Ms. Daly went on to explain that what I did was called an exothermic reaction. How things went from high energy to low energy.

I was definitely not feeling low energy. I couldn't stop grinning.

Oh yeah, chemistry was cool!

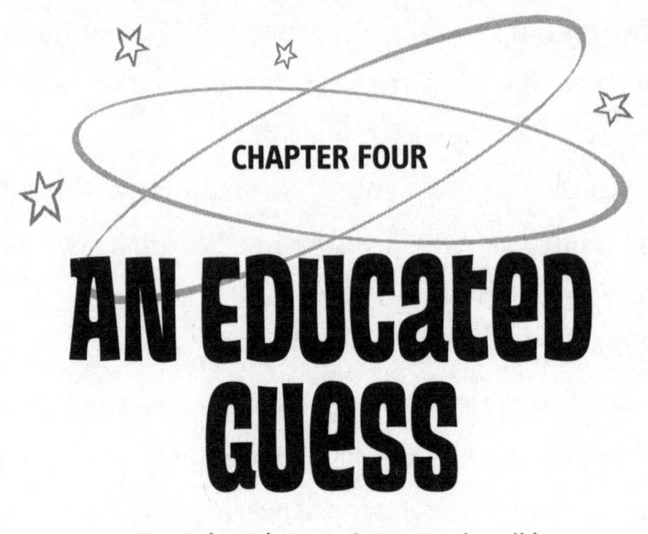

CHAPTER FOUR

AN EDUCATED GUESS

Hypothesis (noun). Sometimes people call it an educated guess. That doesn't mean that a guess is super smart. It just means that you are going to make a prediction based on really checking something out.

"I CAN'T BELIEVE WHAT'S HAPPENING." My fingers furiously tapped on my iPad. "I just popped ten bubbles. At once. I didn't know that was a thing."

"It is a thing," said Birdie, who stood on her head across from me in our family room. Her long black hair spread like a curtain onto the beige carpet. It had been only a day since the fire breathing demo, and I was itching for a new science adventure. But I hadn't come up

with anything. You really can't count Bubble Zap, although I had been practicing a lot, since it was Saturday.

"This is a miracle," I said. "Since I'm awful at Bubble Zap."

"And now you're a legend."

"Wait until we tell Elijah. I'm going to destroy his top score!" *Pop! Pop! Pop!* I continued to rack up points. But a couple of bubbles vanished before I could get them. Then all at once the game was over.

"What?!!! It can't just end. I was so close. This thing is rigged!" I flung the iPad so that it bounced against a pillow, landing with a soft thud on a stack of magazines on the coffee table.

Birdie snapped out of her headstand. "Hey, easy on that." Her face was firework red. The super bright kind made from a gray carbon powder called strontium carbonate. Birdie plopped next to me on the couch. "You never give up on games. What's going on?"

"I should have beaten Elijah's score with those ten bubbles at once." I harrumphed.

"Oh, c'mon. It's just Bubble Zap. It's so dumb they should pay us to play it."

A smile crept onto my face, so I bit my bottom lip. I didn't want Birdie to stop cheering me up. I sighed like my grandma Dort.

"Seriously, what's really up?" asked Birdie softly.

Flopping back against the couch, I tried to figure out the best way to explain that I'd been worrying about fall break camp all week. I really wanted to do it with Birdie and Elijah. But I didn't think there were any choices that all three of us would want to do together. "We can't do chemistry camp during fall break since Ms. Daly will be gone," I said. "But that's the only camp we'd both like. Elijah, too. And I'd miss you if I did math camp while you did art camp."

"*That's* why you're in a bad mood?" Birdie flopped back next to me. "I'd miss you, too! I can't believe Ms. Daly is going away to St. Paul. But I'm sure we can figure out something."

"I mean, Ms. Daly deserves an awesome vacation. But still. Kids need science as much as breathing. I mean, every time we"—I made a gulping sound—"breathe, it's science. Oxygen molecules going in

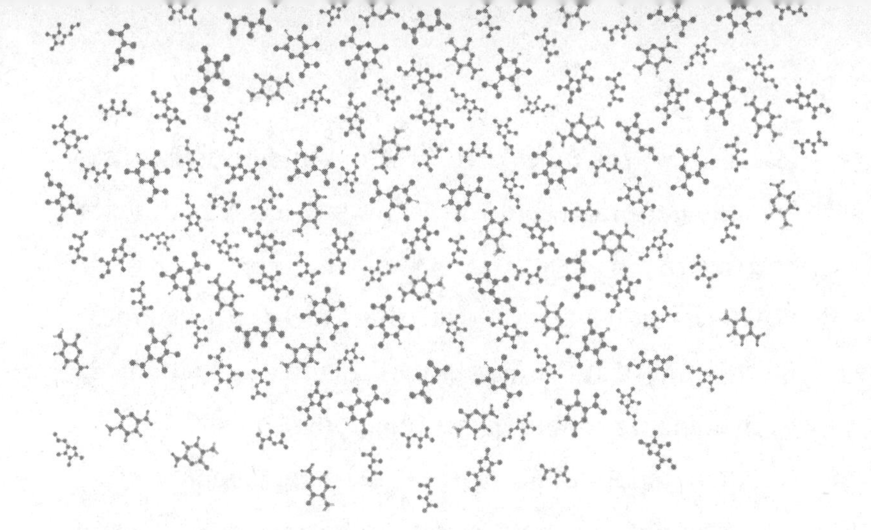

and"—I exhaled—"carbon dioxide molecules going out."

Birdie dramatically puffed out air. "Yup. There go some molecules right now. See ya"—she waved—"have a nice life."

"Not just some molecules. Billions and billions. A whole galaxy."

"Wow," said Birdie. "I never thought of it that way. I'll have to sketch this galaxy."

"You could during fall science camp." I hopped off the couch. "If it existed."

"Wait, maybe you could run camp! If any kid could do that, it'd be you, Kate."

I thought about that. I could totally run a science camp. I knew so many experiments from watching Dr.

Caroline on YouTube. "Hm," I said, pondering the idea. "I could definitely come up with some fun experiments and demos."

"But probably don't do the fire breathing one." Birdie glanced at the fire extinguisher in our kitchen. "It went amazing yesterday. But that poor cactus."

"Good point. But there's a glue demo I could try."

"Ooh, and then we could use it to make a collage!" Birdie said.

I took a deep breath. "Okay, so all I have to do is convince my mom I could lead fall break chemistry camp. Which means I need to get her in a really good mood. You came up with the perfect solution, Birdie!"

Birdie took a bow. "What are best friends for?" she asked.

Pacing back and forth in front of the couch, I talked to myself. "Think, Kate. C'mon. I could wash her car. Except it's already clean. She just waxed it." I tapped my head, trying to think harder. *Tap. Tap. Tap.*

"Are you trying to pop bubbles in your brain?" joked Birdie.

"I sure hope not," I said. "Hey, I got it! Mom just bought a new bag of chocolate pieces. Which means

she is getting ready to bake brownies. But with her grant due, she hasn't had time. We'll make them for her! That's perfect!"

"It'll make me happy, too," said Birdie, licking her lips.

We both jumped together like we were on the trampoline. Then Birdie suddenly stopped. "That's a good sign," she said. "That she bought the chocolate, I mean."

Birdie was big into signs and omens. Not me. The only way to know the future was by testing out a hypothesis, which was basically an educated guess.

Based on the number of bags of semisweet chocolate pieces Mom had purchased in her lifetime, especially when she was worried, I could safely guess she was craving brownies, her absolute favorite dessert. Since last night, she had been holed up in her office working on that grant for a school garden. The deadline was Monday. She wanted to name the garden in honor of a second-grade teacher, Mrs. Farwell, who was retiring this year.

Super chocolaty brownies were definitely the answer. They just had to be.

CHAPTER FIVE

Like MUD

Condensation (noun). A gas turns into a liquid when the conditions are just right. It's like a bunch of molecules at a party, sliding into one another mosh-pit style. Then an electric wand messes with them, and now the molecules are closer together and dancing in unison.

WITH WIDE EYES, Liam studied the bag of semi-sweet chocolate on the counter. And the sugar, eggs, vanilla, flour, cocoa powder, and salt. "What are you making?"

"Brownies," said Birdie.

"Hey, I want to make brownies!" cried Liam.

I put my fingers to my lips. "Shhh, keep your voice down."

Liam squinted. "Is it a 'prise?"

"A *sur*prise," I corrected. "For Mom. She's been working really hard and needs a little treat."

"I could hear you shouting earlier," said Liam. "*You* were loud."

"We shouldn't have been," said Birdie, setting out metal measuring cups.

"I want to make brownies!" Liam grabbed the bag of chocolate pieces.

"You're too little to cook by yourself," I said. Liam was in kindergarten. Mom didn't let me cook by myself until the summer after third grade.

"At school, I'm a paper passer." Liam proudly thumped his chest. "And a line leader."

"Well, now you can be the official taster," I said. "That's the best part of brownie making."

"You get to lick the bowl," explained Birdie.

"But I want to cook!" Liam waved the bag of chocolate. It dropped out of his curled fist, thwacking against the island counter.

"Hey, what's going on in here?" asked Dad, walking in from the basement. That was where he has his woodworking area and spent several hours during the weekends. He glanced at the ingredients on the counter and

then at Liam. “Why don’t we let your sister and Birdie take care of baking? Buddy, I need you to go with me to the grocery store. We’re clear out of milk. And you can’t eat brownies without milk, now can you?” Dad scooped up the car keys from the rack. “Plus, I need a shopping associate. And just maybe you can help pick out some chips.”

“The kind that gets my hands orangey?” Liam stared at his palm. “Or the kind with green flecks?”

“Orange or green. Dealer’s choice.”

“Yes!” As Liam charged to the door, he knocked into our dog’s water bowl. A small puddle spread out on our new kitchen floor.

“I’m on it!” I grabbed a rag and wiped the wood floor.

“Thanks, Kate,” said Dad. “But next time let your brother do it himself.”

“Sure!” I tossed the rag to Liam. “Go for it!”

“You already did the good part,” moaned Liam. “It’s hardly wet now.”

Only my brother would think that wiping up a spill was fun. Once after Liam complained that I got to unload the dishwasher, Dad had said that I made everything look cool since I was five years older. I grabbed a glass of

water and spilled it. “There you go! A huge puddle!” Dad rolled his eyes but didn’t say anything. He was awesome like that.

As Liam wiped, Dad put his hand on my shoulder. “There’s something I want to ask you, girls.” He drew in his eyebrows in a serious discussion face. “I want you to think about this long and hard before answering.”

Birdie and I looked at each other. When it came to very important questions, my dad, a therapist, who asked people the right question to help them figure out their problems, was an expert.

“Cakey or fudgy brownies?” asked Dad.

I laughed, relieved that Dad was just being a goofball. “For brownies, I’m team fudgy.”

“Me too,” said Birdie.

Dad told us that was wonderful news and asked if we needed any brownie-making advice from Mom. In our house, Dad’s the cook, but Mom’s the dessert maker. I’ve helped her make brownies but never made them myself. Still, I told him that I had it covered.

“Baking is sort of like a science experiment,” said Dad, winking at us. “Where you still have to clean up after yourself.”

“It’s only an experiment if we test something out,” I said. “And not just anything, but a hypothesis.”

“I have a hypothesis,” said Dad. “That your brownies are going to be delicious.”

Dad got a big thumbs-up from Birdie and me.

Although after he and Liam left, I wished I had asked if Dad knew where to find Mom’s brownie recipe. It took Birdie and me forever to find what looked like the perfect fudgy recipe on her phone (saved by the bowl of rice that absorbed all the pond water).

Suddenly, Birdie’s phone’s battery icon turned red. “Oh no! It’s running out of power.” Birdie frowned. “Snap! I forgot my charger.” Unfortunately, my parents’ chargers didn’t work with her phone. And I didn’t have a smartphone. Just an old flip one only to be used in an emergency. “Maybe we should look up the recipe on the computer and print it out,” said Birdie.

“Nah.” I tapped my head. “It’s all up here.” I just need to get the ratios right. “Cooking is chemistry!”

I boiled water in a pot like I’d seen Mom do, set a metal bowl on top of it, then stirred up the chocolate

and butter into creamy deliciousness. When we set the smooth melted chocolate onto the counter, it immediately turned into what looked like pebbly mud.

I yowled in frustration.

"What is wrong with it?" shrieked Birdie.

"I don't know!" *Okay. Don't panic*, I told myself. *You can fix this.*

Examining the bottom of the pan, I noticed beads of water—condensation!

"Aha!" said Birdie. "The chocolate seized. It's when chocolate gets all mushy instead of luscious and silky. I saw that once on a cooking show."

"Right. It's because it came into contact with moisture." I slapped my forehead. "I should have thought of that! That's basic chemistry. We've got to start all over again." I glanced up at the clock. It was 4:00 p.m. Dinner would be in one hour because Mom wanted to eat early tonight. She had to be up at the crack of dawn tomorrow for her fitness boot camp class.

I pulled out a clean glass bowl and set it over the pan of boiling water. This time everything had to be perfect.

"The chocolate looks great," I said a few minutes later.

"And smells amazing." Leaning over, Birdie admired the rich walnut-brown color. "Super creamy," she exclaimed.

"And this time, we'll wipe off the condensation right away."

Just as I was about to pull the glass bowl off the stove, it shattered with a loud pop.

Like a rain of hail, broken bits of glass and globs of chocolate hit the floor.

"What's that noise?" asked Mom.

Uh-oh!

CHAPTER SIX

KITCHEN CHEMISTRY

Thermal shock (noun). When a rapid temperature change stresses a material and causes cracks. It's like when you pop out at someone and surprise them, and they totally lose it.

"WHAT JUST HAPPENED HERE?" Wide-eyed, Mom peered around the kitchen.

"Nothing," I said, desperately picking up chocolate-covered glass chips with a cloth towel.

"That's glass," observed Mom.

"Maybe a little," I squeaked. "We were making you brownies. Really fudgy kind. For dessert tonight."

"Oh, honey, you'll have to make sure there's no glass

left anywhere. Liam's always running barefoot. Get the broom out of the closet. And the dustpan. And make sure to—"

"Wear gloves. I know, Mom. It was a total accident."

"I can see." She studied the chocolate spread all over the stove.

I couldn't believe we just messed up like that. Right after wanting to do something nice for Mom. It made me think of entropy, the degree in which molecules can get dispersed. And right now, there was a whole bunch of entropy in this kitchen.

Our dog, Dribble, bounded over to the oven, sniffing. He loved entropy.

"Down, Dribble," scolded Birdie. "You can't have any. Chocolate is bad for dogs."

"I really appreciate you girls making dessert," said Mom. "But why did you have the glass bowl over boiling water? Not smart."

The truth? I just wasn't thinking. But I didn't want to admit that to Mom. Not now. It probably wasn't the ideal time, but maybe I could distract her from the broken glass with Birdie's idea about chemistry camp. "Um, well, it was more than just brownie making," I said. "It

was part of an experiment. And speaking of experiments, during fall break, since Ms. Daly won't be around . . ." As I continued to talk, Birdie kept on giving me this look, like *be quiet.* Only I couldn't be quiet. Once I started talking about chemistry, I couldn't stop, and plus, I was nervous about making Mom mad. "We thought I'd be the perfect person to lead a chemistry camp instead. We could make magnetic slime. And do vinegar and baking soda explosions. Nothing would be dangerous. All of it would be fun."

"I'm sure it'd be fun." Mom eyed the gloppy bubbly chocolate and shards of glass still left near the burner. "But no."

I moaned. "C'mon, Mom. There's nothing else that both Birdie and I like to do—Elijah, too. And we want to spend fall break together."

"I guess you'll just have to think of something else." She opened the fridge to grab a bottle of ginger kombucha, a fizzy drink that's supposed to be good for your health, unlike soda.

"Hey, could I borrow a kombucha?" I asked. "It's fermented. It'd be great for an experiment."

"It's my last one. You'll have to find something else, Kate." Mom glanced at the clock on the microwave. "My deadline awaits. Good luck, girls. Make sure you get all the chocolate off the stove, too." My mom was used to my messes—at least she knew I was a good cleaner-upper.

After Mom went back into the office, Birdie sighed. "That didn't go so well. Don't worry, Kate. We can still make brownies and figure out what do during break. What about doing drama camp?"

I pictured my face full of stage makeup, hot lights burning on my cheeks all while I had to figure out how to spin in the same direction as everyone else. "I'm just not good at being onstage like that."

"But you were great breathing fire! And theater camp is going to be *Dragons vs. Unicorns*, a short one-act musical. Mrs. Hansberry wrote it, and it'll be performed for the first time ever at the end of fall break. Unicorns. Honestly. Can it get any better? If you're a dragon, maybe you could even breathe fire."

I thought about that for a moment. "One teensy problem," I said. "I'm not really good at singing or acting . . . and especially not dancing." I bent over to pick

up the dustpan I was using and dumped the glass into the trash can.

"Let's hear you sing, 'Happy Birthday,'" Birdie said as she got a sponge to clean up some spattered chocolate.

I stopped by the sink and belted it out. My voice came out screechy and awful.

"Okay." Birdie plugged her ears. "You're right. Maybe you're not the best singer. What if you just mouthed the words?"

I sighed. "Elijah's coming over after dinner. Maybe he'll have some other fall break camp ideas."

"It'll be okay," Birdie said, patting my shoulder. "The important thing is we're going to get to spend a whole five days together. We'll figure out something."

I hoped she was right.

CHAPTER SEVEN

Leaving It Up to Chance

Gas (noun). The molecules have moved farther apart than in a solid or a liquid. They are like bumper cars ramming into one another, completely out of control.

AFTER DINNER—AND DELICIOUS brownies that Birdie and I managed to get perfectly fudgy—Elijah, Birdie, and I jumped on the trampoline in my backyard.

"We're out-of-control gas molecules," I shouted, throwing my arms wildly and slamming into Birdie, who giggled and plugged her nose like we were stinky.

"Does everything have to be about chemistry?" asked Elijah. "Like, couldn't we just be kids jumping on a trampoline?"

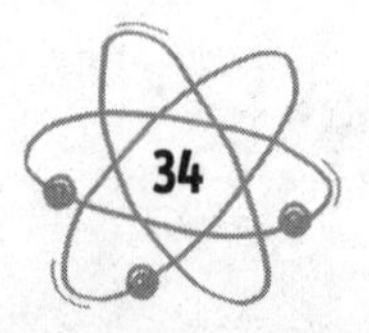

Birdie stuck out her tongue. "Boring! Don't you ever pretend that you're something else when you're practicing the drums?"

"No," said Elijah. "That would be weird."

"Can you two stop it?" I said, plopping myself down on the trampoline. "I want to have a very important conversation: What fall break camp are we going to do together? Don't you think the robotics club sounds cool?"

Birdie made a face and plopped down next to me. "My sister did that one a few years ago and brought the stuff home. I already know everything they're going to do. So, no thanks."

"Hey, I've got an idea!" Elijah picked up the info sheet and then tossed it so it fluttered, settling near the netting of the trampoline. "The writer's workshop. That's what we should do."

"Uh-uh." I shook my head. "Too much sitting. It's break. It has to be fun." I popped up and did a front flip, landing next to my friends. "Something cool."

"How about cheer club?" said Birdie.

"Veto!" Elijah gave a thumbs-down. "I can't do a very good cartwheel. Or a backflip."

"Me either," I said. "Hey, what about the LEGO camp? That might be okay."

"Agreed," said Elijah.

"Not agreed." Birdie crossed her arms. "I don't want to sit around and watch you two fight it out. With Kate obsessed with following the directions and Elijah tossing them."

I laughed at a recent memory. "Yeah, remember when Elijah built some space station using random parts from the rain forest kit?"

"And you had a meltdown," Elijah reminded me.

"Ugh. A definite no!" Birdie rolled her eyes.

"What about drama?" Elijah spread out his arms like he was about to give a monologue.

"Not you, too!" I groaned.

"It's not just about acting and dancing and singing," said Birdie. "They need people to paint the sets, run the spotlights, and open the curtains. Oh, and one really organized fifth grader to be the assistant director. That could be you, Kate! You're the most organized fifth grader ever!"

"I am?" Okay, suddenly I was, maybe, just a little intrigued.

"So it's a deal!" shouted Elijah. "We're all going to go out for the musical?"

Birdie squealed. "The show is sooo good! This one unicorn meets a dragon, and they become friends. But the other unicorns don't like that, and neither do the dragons. In the end, the unicorn and dragon BFFs show everyone that they have more in common than they thought, and the rest of the dragons and unicorns all do a final number together."

It did actually sound a little cool.

"I want to be the lead unicorn," said Birdie, tossing her hair like it was a mane.

"I want to be in charge of lights," said Elijah. "If I flash them back and forth, I can make it look like a lightning storm."

"Maybe I *could* be director," I said.

"Assistant director," corrected Birdie. "Mrs. Hansberry is the director."

"Right." I suddenly felt a little glimmer of hope that maybe there was something about drama that might suit me.

"It's a perfect plan," said Birdie.

It was . . . as long as we all got the positions we wanted.

CHAPTER EIGHT

All the World's a Stage

Law (noun). In science, a law explains a cause and effect that is always the same under the same conditions. It is accepted as true. So if someone makes a goal every time they play soccer—that could be a law!

"WHAT IF I DON'T GET assistant director?" I said.

Birdie squinted at me as we sat together in the school auditorium a little over a week after we had decided to do drama camp. It was Monday morning and the first day of fall break. "You not get assistant director? Um. That's not possible. You really are the best one for the job." While Mrs. Hansberry had everyone audition for a speaking role on Friday, we wrote down our info on a sheet if we

wanted to be part of the stage crew and what our qualifications were. I ended up needing a second sheet to explain why I thought I'd be a good assistant director.

"I'm sure when Mrs. Hansberry heard me sing during auditions, she knew I couldn't be in the cast," I said, "but maybe she could just give me a different crew job." I was worried. "Nothing is for certain." In science, laws are widely accepted as true. And there was no law saying that I was going to be assistant director.

"Look, Kate. It has to be someone organized. Check. Someone who doesn't mind telling other people what to do. Check. Someone who can keep track of many things at once. Check. The assistant director position has your name all over it. And you submitted such a good application!"

"Seriously. What if I don't get it?"

"Then you'll do something else," said Birdie, who sat next to me in the second row. In front of us sat Avery and Phoenix while Elijah sat with his friend Jeremy Rowe in the aisle across the way. We were all waiting for Mrs. Hansberry to announce who got what part or position for the musical. About two dozen other kids sat in the seats also waiting.

I guess being prop master could be okay. That was my second choice. But it wasn't as good as assistant director. I glanced at the sleek leather backpack by my feet. My mom let me borrow her leather bag. I had packed an emergency theater supply kit so big I couldn't get my regular backpack to close. My emergency kit included thick rope, two bottles of water, tape, glue, a measuring tape, and scissors. I wanted to be prepared.

"I really hope we both get what we want," Birdie whispered.

"You will," I told her. "You're an amazing singer. Even when you're upside down!"

Birdie blushed. She's not very good at compliments. "Uh, thanks."

"You deserve the lead unicorn. Seriously. There is nobody in the entire fifth grade who knows more about them. And if—"

"Shhh," said Birdie, pointing to the stage, which was completely empty. "Mrs. Hansberry's coming. I heard her voice."

"Right." Birdie has super good hearing. She can hear my dad snoring when she spends the night, even when we spread out in sleeping bags downstairs in the basement.

"Hey," I said, leaning over to look at Birdie's drawing. "Can I see?"

She snapped shut her drawing pad.

"Aw, c'mon, Birdie." All I caught a glimpse of was where she had signed her name—Brinda Bhatt. She always signed her art with her real name. Birdie was just a nickname. "I'm sure it's fantabulous and could be framed in a museum."

She stuffed the pad into her backpack. "Another time."

She was such an amazing artist. Every year since we were five, she had drawn me a handmade birthday card. I kept them all in a box under my bed. But sometimes she was private about her artwork.

Kids murmured and pointed as Mrs. Hansberry made her way to the front of the stage. Like always, she

was dressed dramatically. This afternoon, she wore a bright green shawl and long dangly earrings in the shape of theater masks.

"I'm going to announce roles and positions," said Mrs. Hansberry, "so if I could please have your attention."

Actually, Mrs. Hansberry didn't need to say that last part. The place was as silent as outer space. I couldn't wait to hear what she was about to say.

CHAPTER NINE

STUCK ON YOU

Polymers (noun). Big molecules made from a bunch of smaller molecules. They're like a soccer team that sticks together.

"THANK YOU, BOYS AND GIRLS," said Mrs. Hansberry. "I was so impressed with your auditions. You all showed quite a bit of enthusiasm. And, frankly, this decision was not an easy one. In truth, any one of you could have played any of the innumerable roles, large or small." Her eyes swept the auditorium, and, for a moment, they landed on mine.

No. No. Please. I don't want a part. Or innumerable roles. Sheesh. Mrs. Hansberry loved to use big words. She said if you don't know what something means, then go look it up.

Suddenly, someone was shaking me. It was Birdie. "Did you hear? I got the part! I'm the lead unicorn!"

I hugged her and gave a high five and a big loud yay.

Then Birdie was shushing me. "Some other people wanted that part, too," she said, lowering her voice. "We don't want them to feel bad. Since we all have to work together as a cast and crew."

Right. Kind of like a polymer. A giant molecule made up of a bunch of smaller ones. Of course, there was nothing wrong with showing my happiness for my BFF. My dad the therapist said if you deny your emotions, it meant you could get messed up. "Own it," I said.

Mrs. Hansberry announced a bunch of other parts, as well as all of the tech positions. When she explained that Elijah would do the lights, he hooted. And Jeremy slapped him hard on the back and whispered something to him.

"And Kate's going to be our assistant director."

"Yes!" I whooped. In front of me, Avery sniffed as if I were being too rambunctious, but I didn't care.

Anyway, Mrs. Hansberry didn't seem to mind. She motioned me forward. "Kate, can you stand up?"

I bounced out of my seat and gave a quick wave.

"Kate will be assisting me and generally helping to keep rehearsal running smoothly," said Mrs. Hansberry. "She will be my second pair of eyes. So that's it, children. However, I'm going to need some volunteers to help pass out the scripts."

Mrs. Hansberry handed me a small stack of scripts. "We're going to have great fun working together," she said with a wide smile.

"Definitely! Do you have a list of my duties?" I asked.

"You're just going to have to follow my lead, and we'll make it up as we go along. I've never used a student assistant director before, so this is a first." She winked. "I think you'll do a terrific job."

As I passed out the scripts, my stomach twisted. The actors had scripts and lines to follow. They had a set of directions as clear as steps to an experiment posted by Dr. Caroline. What did I get? I was supposed to make things up as I went along.

What if I didn't know what to do? What if my making it up was all wrong?

As I handed a script to some of the kids who were cast as dragons, Elijah put out his hand. "Hello. I need a script, too!"

"What do you mean?" I asked.

"Not just unicorns and dragons get scripts. I need to follow the script for the light cues."

"Of course." I handed Elijah a script. "I knew that."

"Yeah, right." Elijah squinted at me. "And unicorns are real. Along with singing dragons. They live in the land of happy rainbows."

"Ha-ha," I admitted. Then I whispered, "Okay, I seriously didn't know about the lighting cues."

"I know," said Elijah.

"I'm making this up as I go."

"We can tell," said Jeremy, who had one of the lead dragon roles, along with Julia and Rory Workman.

"Just don't make up lines," I warned. "I'll be checking the script."

"Now I'm scared," said Jeremy in a mock quivery voice.

"Good," I said, then marched away, wondering, Could I do this? Could I make this up as I went along? I really didn't know.

During a break, after doing a read-through, I hurried to Birdie to see how she was doing. "I don't think Avery is very happy," she said, pointing over to where she was

frowning at her script. “She’s only got three lines. Bet she was hoping to be lead dragon. Even though she’s great as dance captain. They say she’s the best in her jazz class at Dance Academy.” Avery was always saying how her dance class helped her soccer skills. She was definitely sure-footed on the field.

“She’s so perfect as one of the dancing dragons,” I said. Those were the dragons without big speaking parts. They sang a couple of songs and had two dance numbers.

After the morning break, we sat around in a circle on the stage and talked about how the read-through went.

I noticed that Birdie’s voice wasn’t loud enough. But I figured it was too early to say something. It’s not like there was an audience yet.

Jeremy said that we should work hard on keeping it realistic.

“What do you mean by that?” I asked.

“The dragons need to be intimidating,” he said. “If we do it just for laughs, it won’t be as much fun. We’ve got to scare the first graders a little bit.” He snarled and roared.

And a few kids screamed.

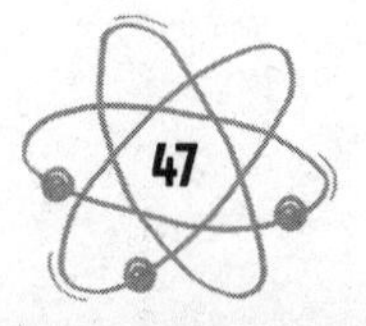

“Like that,” said Jeremy.

“He has a point,” said Mrs. Hansberry. “That can be something for us to work on.”

That gives me an idea. “We can have the dragons breathe real fire!”

“Did you say real live fire, my dear?” asked Mrs. Hansberry.

“Yeah! Like Jeremy says, it will make it more realistic and scare people. A lot.”

Mrs. Hansberry swept her arms dramatically over her face. “I’m afraid it will be too much of a real scare for the audience—and for your director.”

My mind sifted through all the shows I’ve watched on Dr. Caroline’s YouTube channel where she made stuff explode. “Hey, what about lycopodium powder?”

“Oh, well, that sounds vaguely familiar,” said Mrs. Hansberry. “Please tell me more.”

“It’s what circus performers use to blow fire. It looks like the dust on my dad’s workbench. And it’s supposed to work really well.”

“Aha! I’m not so sure I know enough about it. The circus performer part sounds a bit intimidating. So for now, I’m going to give you a conditional no. But I prom-

ise to look it up when I get home. We need a very safe yet exciting solution."

"What if we use smoke instead of fire? We could project a video of smoke onto a screen . . ."

"Hmm." Mrs. Hansberry squinted her eyes. "Now, that's a creative solution. What if our dragons exhale blizzards instead of fire?"

"Is that scary enough?" asked Elijah almost to himself.

Avery shot up her hand. "My parents use special effects all of the time at their theater. At Brookside, we have a theatrical fog machine."

"That's an excellent idea," said Mrs. Hansberry. "What do you think, Kate?"

"You know how in winter your breath looks like smoke because it is cold? I think it should look like that. But I don't think this will look *enough* like that," I admitted, feeling bad about vetoing Avery's idea but also wanting to tell the truth and make the show look the best it could be.

"You don't know how the special effects will look." Avery turned around and rolled her eyes.

"We may have some other options," I said. "Let me think on this."

"Good luck with that," said Avery.

I didn't need luck. I just needed my brain. And Dr. Caroline's list of experiments.

Tomorrow we would go over blocking. Those were the directions for where everyone needed to be onstage and when they moved. Honestly, before this afternoon I had never heard that word. Mrs. Hansberry told me that it would be my job to take notes into the director's script. "I've marked it up pretty well, but I always like to make some in-the-moment adjustments," she told me.

"Got it!"

"I know you will," she said.

After we had a lunch break and completed some group bonding exercises (we had to do tongue twisters together), I went to pick up my mom's leather backpack. Immediately, I noticed that my zipper was open.

"That's funny," I said to Birdie. "I remember zipping it."

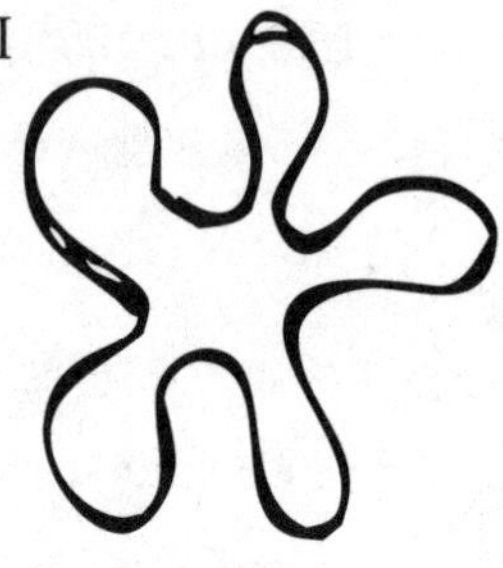

Curiously, I peered inside my bag. Globs of something waxy and blobby dotted the inside. "What's that?" I screeched.

CHAPTER TEN

A SCIENCE SPELL

Liquid (noun). The molecules are waving their arms and sidestepping because they have more space than they do when they're a solid. Like the difference between chocolate milk and brownies, sort of.

CHOCOLATE MILK

IT WAS MY FAULT. I hadn't tightened the cap on the bottle of glue in Mom's bag. I had checked, and it had been loose. Now I had to deal with a sticky mess. In the family room after play rehearsal, Liam and I watched *Dr. Caroline*.

Normally, I love *Dr. Caroline*. Normally, I binge-watch it. But today, my mind was completely stuck on the globs of glue wedged inside Mom's bag.

To make things worse, Mom clanked around the kitchen, scrubbing the sink. Which meant she was stressed.

Which meant I had to wait until she was gone before digging under the sink to find something to clean her bag.

"Look! Dr. Caroline is doing something dangerous," cried Liam, waving at a tub of boiling liquid nitrogen on the computer screen.

This was one of my favorite experiments. Basically, Dr. Caroline dunked balloon animals into chilly liquid nitrogen. Actually, super-freezing—as in four times colder than the North Pole in the middle of a blizzard.

"Will she get hurt?" asked Liam, a little too enthusiastically.

"Don't worry. She's got extra-special gloves. Plus, she's wearing goggles and a lab coat."

In the kitchen, Mom rinsed out all of the soap in the sink. Hopefully, she would scoot into her office really soon.

"Hey, Dr. Caroline's doing a spell!" said Liam, fixing his eyes on the computer screen. The balloon animals shriveled like raisins when they hit the sizzling liquid nitrogen. When Dr. Caroline scooped them out of the tub, they blew back up again.

"It looks like magic, but it's just science." Charles' Law to be specific. As the temperature dropped, the

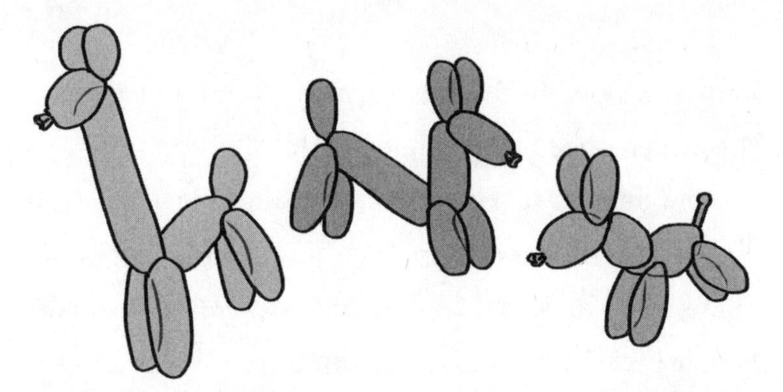

volume went down, causing the balloons to shrink. As temperature rose, the volume increased, causing the balloons to plump back up again.

Mom stopped running the water. "Kids," she called out, glancing down at her phone. "Good news. I just found out that the school's a finalist for that community grant I applied for."

"Yay!" cried out Liam.

"I knew it!" I said.

Humming happily, Mom polished the sink with a soft dry cloth. "They're going to interview me tomorrow. I want to bring in those scrapbooks showing off the school garden. The grant committee can visualize our farm-to-table lunch program."

"Our school's turning into a farm?" asked Liam, bouncing off the couch.

"Well, sort of." Mom folded up the cloth. "Kids can

harvest veggies. In the fall, the plan is to eat lunch from the garden once a week. That is, if we win the grant."

"I want to be a harvest kid," exclaimed Liam.

"You can!" Mom hung her gloves under the sink. "Kate, you know that leather backpack you borrowed? I'd like it back for the meeting tomorrow. It'd be perfect to load up with the scrapbooks."

"Sure," I said, hoping my warm face wasn't giving away my inner panic. What should I do? Tell her the truth? Her happiness would shrivel up faster than the liquid nitrogen balloon. Plus, she would think I was irresponsible. "Um, it's in my room. The bag, I mean. I'll get it for you in a sec."

My throat swelled with worry.

Normally, my mom thought I was pretty responsible, which is why she let me do lots of stuff on my own. But after last week's glass bowl explosion in the kitchen and now the glue in the backpack, I wasn't so sure. Maybe she would tell Mrs. Hansberry I shouldn't be the assistant director. Then I couldn't be with Birdie or Elijah.

"I'm sorry to snatch that bag back." Mom strolled over to the couch. "I feel terrible."

"Oh, don't. Seriously." I rubbed my chin. "But . . .

maybe you could use a more official-looking bag. Like a briefcase?"

"Hmmm. I thought about that, but it'd look too corporate. Like the school doesn't need the money. A nice backpack is perfect."

Actually, her backpack was the opposite of perfect right now.

"Thanks, honey." Mom kissed my forehead and then Liam's cheek. "You guys are the best—just sitting there watching a science show." She clasped her hands, beaming down at us. "How did I ever get so lucky?"

I opened my mouth to tell her that she didn't get that lucky, but my lips stuck together as if they'd been glued.

As soon as Mom left, I barreled into the kitchen.

"Hey," said Liam. "Can we do that Dr. Caroline spearmint together?"

"It's called an experiment. And no, it's too dangerous without a grown-up around and the proper gear. But I have another experiment, and it's called cleaning. Want to try?"

"No way!"

That's exactly what I thought, and what I was counting on.

CHAPTER ELEVEN

ONE STEP CLOSER

Solutes (noun). Substances that dissolve.
Like what happens to cocoa powder when you pour steaming milk (called a solvent) to make hot cocoa.

MAYBE I COULD PLOP the backpack into the freezer. If the glue froze, I might be able to break it off the fabric lining with my hands. Or I could use a knife to peel it away.

When I opened the freezer, I saw ice cream, frozen peas, burritos, and Popsicles. Unfortunately, Dad had just gone shopping at Costco. The freezer was jam-packed and there wasn't enough room for the bag.

As my grandma Dort would say, now it was time for me to face the music. Or rather the glue.

I yanked out the bottle of Elmer's from the bag and read the label. It said it was water soluble.

The glue would soften like butter if I got it wet.

After filling our kettle with water, I set the bag on the counter. A bit later, I poured warm water onto a rag, and then attacked a glob of glue.

Total fail.

Disgusted, I slammed the wet rag into the perfect, shiny, Mom-cleaned sink.

Then I realized something. In science, when you eliminate one thing, you are one step closer to the solution.

A fail was a win.

CHAPTER TWELVE

ACCIDENTS HAPPEN

Solution (noun). When a solvent (milk) dissolves a solute (cocoa powder), you create a solution. In this case, a solution is something you drink, not an answer to a math problem.

THE WARM WATER DIDN'T DO THE TRICK.

I paced. I tapped my head. *Think, Kate. Think. Think!*

Wait a minute. Instead of just thinking, I needed to gather evidence. Make observations. This time I opened the bag all the way and set it under the bright lights on the kitchen counter. I could see that some of the glue had softened. But not enough.

Maybe I just needed to keep the hot rag on the glue longer.

This time, I let the glue soften with the rag for a long time. A while later, it was time to test out my hypothesis. When I checked the bag, I was able to rinse it all off!

Yes. Yes. Yes. My hunch had been right. But now the fabric was all wet.

Racing upstairs to the bathroom, I grabbed a hair dryer from the cabinet. Liam knocked around in his bedroom. After I had mentioned cleaning earlier, he had escaped upstairs.

"What are you doing?" he called out.

"Nothing," I lied as I hustled back downstairs. Well, not exactly a lie. Because after my cleaning and drying, I would be doing nothing.

As the hair dryer roared on, Mom stepped into the kitchen. "What's going on in here?" Her eyes lasered on her bag spread open on the kitchen counter. And the hair dryer.

I turned off the dryer. "Your bag got a little wet. And gluey. But I took care of it."

"Oh, Kate." Her eyebrows knitted together in concern. "I had hoped you'd be more responsible. That you were old enough to take care of the bag."

"Mom, I'm super sorry! It was an accident."

"You have to think. You can't always be in such a rush."

I was going to protest. But I was the one who didn't check to see if the bottle of glue in my emergency kit had been closed tightly.

"I'd like an explanation," Mom said in her firm principal voice. It was too eerily calm. Her dark brown eyes bored into mine, like she could read my thoughts. If Mom had a superpower, it would definitely be mind reading.

I blurted out everything that had happened. How I had discovered the gluey mess in her backpack. How upset I had been. How much I had wanted to tell her, but she had seemed so happy about the grant. "Don't worry," I said, trying to sound 100 percent more confident than I felt. "It'll be fine."

Her eyes took in the darkened spots on the lining. "Really?"

"Okay, maybe not perfect. But almost."

Mom combed her fingers through her hair. It was super short with blonde highlights. Once she became principal last year, she said she didn't want to fuss with

her long hair. That meant she didn't want any extra problems.

Right now, I was her problem. I hated disappointing her in any way. I blinked back tears. "I'm so sorry, Mom. Really. I hope this doesn't hurt your chances."

"No, I'm sorry. I didn't mean to lash out. It's just that I counted on you being careful. Oh, honey." She placed her hand on my shoulder. "It's always something, isn't it? Thanks for making such an effort to clean it up. I'm sure it'll be dry by the morning." Furrowing her brow, she inspected the lining. "The grant committee won't be inspecting the inside of the bag anyway. In the future, just try to keep things safer."

"I will. You can count on it!"

Mom pulled me in for a hug. She smelled like coffee and sweet cream. She always knew how to make me feel better.

Soon after project bag cleanup, Birdie came over and asked if I wanted to ride bikes.

Of course I did!

After I caught her up on the conversation with Mom, we rode over to Oak Bend Pond. It was the perfect antidote to what happened. Being outside in nature always calms me down. Setting our bikes against a large oak tree, I noticed that the trees had changed colors. When I squinted my eyes, the gold, red, and orange leaves looked like dancing flames in the wind. As the branches swayed, I heard blue jays chittering.

The breeze picked up and blew ripples across the pond.

When you think pond, you might get the wrong idea. It was actually a medium-sized lake—forty-two feet deep and over three hundred acres. There were deer, fox and herons, owls and muskrats. Tall silvery cattails framed the shoreline.

"I love this place," I said, picking up a speckled rock to skip. It felt smooth and cool in my hand.

"Me too," said Birdie, sighing happily. "Didn't you think the play read-through went well?"

"Yes, definitely."

"Good. I just wish Avery wasn't so cranky about being dragon dance captain. It makes no sense. It's a

good part. Two songs and two dances. Plus, she's doing the choreography."

"Maybe she's in a bad mood because her braces got tightened," I said. "In soccer practice, she was complaining about it."

"Yeah, could be."

"I know Avery's parents have that fog smoke machine thingy, but I'm going to figure out how to make dragons breathe smoke. So it looks like it's spurting out of their mouths."

"You could really do that?" asked Birdie, her eyes wide.

"I think so."

"That would be *so* cool." Birdie picked up a flat gray pebble, perfect for skipping.

"Thanks for forcing me to do the play. I think it's going to be fun. Even if it meant I got my mom's bag full of glue."

"You're welcome," said Birdie, who skipped her rock so it zigzagged across the lake. "Now, that's a good sign," she said with a wink.

CHAPTER THIRTEEN

Always Break a Leg

Probability (noun). The likelihood that something will happen. It's the odds that when you flip a coin it will be heads or tails. Or the chances of you winning in rock, paper, scissors.

FIRST THING IN THE MORNING on Tuesday, I pulled out the rehearsal schedule and stuffed my backpack under a seat.

"I put my glue in a sealed bag today," I said to Birdie. "Wish me luck!"

"No, Kate! Take that back!"

"What do you mean?"

"It's bad luck to say"—she lowered her voice—"*good luck* in a theater. You're supposed to say *break a leg*."

"Oh, c'mon. That's silly. There's no such thing as luck. It's all probability. If you roll two dice, there's a higher chance you'll get a seven than a two. Superstitions are plain weird. They make people do weird stuff like hate on black cats or run into a busy street to get away from a ladder." I grabbed Birdie's arm. "So, I'm going to say *good luck*, just to myself—since you're so against it."

Birdie clapped her hands over her ears. "Please. Stop. Now something bad is definitely going to happen. I'm really afraid."

For a moment, I thought she was joking. But judging from her quivery bottom lip, she wasn't.

"Look, the only bad thing that's going to happen is we're going to be late to start rehearsal." I was supposed to go over the schedule with the cast, while Mrs. Hansberry organized the backstage crew. It was part of my job.

In the back of the theater, Mrs. Hansberry motioned me over. Today, she was dressed in a longish skirt and Birkenstocks with rainbow socks. Immediately, I felt too plain in my jeans and pink T-shirt. Tomorrow, I decided, I was going to dress with more flair. That would be fun. Putting my schedule on the seat, I

hurried toward Mrs. Hansberry while Birdie headed to sit with the rest of the cast in the first two rows of the theater.

"Here's the prop list," said Mrs. Hansberry, handing me a paper. "It's good to have props as early as possible so actors can rehearse with them."

"That makes sense." It was a long list with items like a crystal orb, an oversize dragon sandwich, blankets, and a long jump rope to tie up the unicorns.

"I'm going to be at least thirty minutes with the crew. We'll be with Mr. Caldera, the facility manager, discussing some basic safety procedures. I trust that you can take care of the cast rehearsal schedule. Who needs to be where and when."

"Of course! I've got it under control."

Mrs. Hansberry glanced over at the first two rows where all the actors were in the process of sitting down and nodded. "Splendid. This is the only time that Mr. Caldera can meet, and I want to be respectful of his schedule."

I took that as Mrs. Hansberry's polite hint that she needed to go.

When I turned around, Birdie was still walking

toward the first two rows of seats. That was so Birdie. She acted as if she had all day to do everything.

I hurried back to my seat where I had placed the schedule. When I peered down at the sheet, I let out a small squeal. Black streaks of ink blotted out all the information. What was going on here?! Someone had used a Sharpie to cross out everything I needed to know.

This definitely wasn't some sort of dumb accident. This was on purpose.

CHAPTER FOURTEEN

SLIP SLIDING AWAY

Vapor (noun). A gas formed by boiling a liquid.
Like if you boil water and watch the steam hover above the pot.

THE ACTORS SAT IN THE FIRST two rows of the auditorium waiting for me to tell them the schedule.

Only I couldn't help them. Not when all the information had been crossed out! I didn't have time to figure out who had played this joke on me. The neurons in my brain had to fire speedy quick to find a solution.

"Kate!" said Avery. "Everyone's ready."

"Hold on one second!" I called out. "Just have to get something!"

Mrs. Hansberry had written the schedule with a ballpoint pen in her elegant cursive handwriting. As quickly as possible, I ran a pencil over the back of the page to get the raised letters to appear.

Then I pulled out a little mirror that I had in my bag. When I looked in the mirror, the letters faced in the right direction.

Yes, I could read the schedule now! Victory!

Sprinting up front, I began explaining what was happening when. "The main dragon roles should go over their lines in the green room." I paused, searching around the auditorium for a green room. The seats were brown. The walls were beige. There was nothing green in sight. "Um, what's the green room?"

"You don't know what a green room is?" asked Jeremy in a shocked voice.

I bit my lip. Everyone could definitely tell I didn't know what I was doing.

"A green room is where actors hang out before a show," explained Avery. "At my dads' theater, it's large with a snack machine."

"Um, okay." My stomach twisted. How could I help direct if I didn't even know the basics? "So the main uni-

corns should go over their lines in the back rows, while the dragon and the unicorn dance teams will work on their choreography onstage. And if you're playing a bunch of smaller roles, go meet in the prop room."

As everyone started to leave, Avery held up her hand. "There's something important I've got to do." She opened her bag and rummaged around inside. Then she grabbed a bottle of glue with one hand and lifted it out so she could get to something underneath. A bag of Starbursts. "Catch!" she said, tossing out dozens of candies.

"You can do that anytime," said Jeremy, snagging four or five fruit chews, and Avery smiled widely.

Some of the actors who didn't get any looked bummed. Especially Birdie.

"Next time, maybe you should hand them out," I said. "So everyone gets one." My eyes met Birdie's.

"It was just for fun," said Phoenix. "Why are you making such a big deal about it?"

"It's good to be fair," said Birdie quietly.

Wow. I never thought being assistant director would be this hard.

While dragons and unicorns ran through dance steps, I sat in the front row, figuring out how to get the

dragons to breathe smoke. I wanted it to look as if the smoke curled right out the dragons' mouths. But how?

Up onstage, thumping feet echoed through the theater.

"Shake your foot in the air," said Avery who was taking her role as dance captain seriously. Maybe a little too seriously. Her voice sounded irritated. "And now slap your foot on the floor even harder. That's the first part of the box step."

A few of the boys stomped so hard, some kids jumped back in surprise.

Groaning dramatically, Avery threw up her hands in exasperation. "The dancing shouldn't scare people."

Hmm, the fake smoke should at least be a little scary and surprising, but not dangerous.

Jogging up and down the aisle, I pretended to dribble a soccer ball. Somehow I needed to jumpstart my brain.

Avery continued with her directions. "Remember the weight is on the right leg," she said. "Shake the left foot."

Jeremy started singing "The Hokey Pokey" and some of the kids giggled.

“That’s not such a bad idea,” said Julia, who was one of the lead dragons.

“It’s not part of the choreography,” said Avery in a tight voice.

A group of boys wiggled their arms Hokey Pokey–style, and Avery frowned.

“Save the Hokey Pokey. Otherwise, exit stage right,” I called out.

“It’s stage left,” said Avery. I suddenly remembered just now that stage directions were from the actors’ point of view. Not the audience’s. Mrs. Hansberry had explained this to us yesterday. “And I’ve got it under control.” Avery put her hands on her hips. “I don’t need your help.”

“Of course,” I said, trying to sound like Mrs. Hansberry.

After a few more tries, Avery was finally able to show everyone how to cross over their right foot. Which didn’t seem that hard but was very challenging to Rory and Jeremy, who kept messing up and crossing their left.

After I came back from checking on how the actors were doing in the green room (better than the dance team), I sat down in the back of the auditorium to do

some thinking. I was itching for my dad's phone so I could watch *Dr. Caroline* and get some ideas for dragon smoke.

The shriveled balloon demo came to mind. Then I remembered Dr. Caroline's special smoking Cheetos that had been dipped in liquid nitrogen. When she chomped on one, it looked like smoke shot right out of her mouth and nose. Only it was just a cloud of the water vaporizing.

But there was one big problem. If liquid nitrogen was used incorrectly, it could burn someone's throat or mouth. Sort of like frostbite, only without being in the cold. Still, liquid nitrogen was the most awesome thing ever. It was powerful. It made balloons shrink. It could be used to freeze off warts (yuck!). And yes, it would make the absolutely perfect pretend smoke.

Bouncing in my seat, I imagined all of the amazing vapor that formed as the liquid nitrogen became a gas. That always happens at its boiling point. Just like water becomes steam.

But how could I make it safe enough for Mrs. Hansberry to say it would be okay to use?

Maybe we could use sticks to spear the Cheetos. The dragons could blow on them to encourage the nitrogen to evaporate. That way they wouldn't have any of their skin or body parts touching the liquid nitrogen.

To be extra safe, I would need those special blue cryogenic gloves that Dr. Caroline used. Somehow, I had to convince Mom and Dad to get me gloves as a very, very early birthday present.

As I pushed out of my seat, I stepped on a piece of watermelon-scented chewing gum. "Ugh!" I moaned.

First the blacked-out rehearsal schedule, then messing up stage right and stage left, and now gum! This was not my day.

I would have to de-gum my shoe with some peanut butter (because: chemistry) when I got home. But, more importantly, I was going to figure out who had spit that gum in front of my seat. Was it on purpose? And if it was, was it the same person who scribbled all over my rehearsal schedule? Now I was going to have to be a scientist, an assistant director, and a detective.

CHAPTER FIFTEEN

SOMETHING STINKS!

Protocol (noun). A set of instructions so you can re-create an experiment or procedure. You can make up ridiculous songs, but you never want to make up ridiculous protocols in science.

AFTER PUTTING A SMALL PIECE OF paper on my shoe so I wouldn't get gum everywhere, I raced up to Mrs. Hansberry as she left the lighting booth. "I figured it out!" I cried.

"The play?" She glanced up from her clipboard. "Life? What, pray tell?"

I loved how Mrs. Hansberry sounded so old-

fashioned and elegant. As if she had stepped out of a Shakespeare play or something.

"How we can get the dragons to breathe out smoke during the finale. So it looks like it's coming out of their mouths and nostrils." And then words zipped out of my mouth as I explained my liquid nitrogen Cheeto concept. How we could make it completely safe using every sort of safety protocol. A protocol is a set of instructions that tell you the right way to do something, and with liquid nitrogen you couldn't afford to do it the wrong way.

"This is most intriguing, Kate," said Mrs. Hansberry, closing her eyes as if she were imagining the possibilities. "However, this is something I would need to discuss over the phone with Ms. Daly and a few others, such as your wonderful mother. But if we follow the safety protocol and give this privilege to a few dragons who are utterly up for the responsibility, we might be able to give this a green light."

As I started jumping up and down, Avery shuffled past us loudly chewing gum. She plopped down in a seat on the aisle next to Phoenix.

The minute I ended the conversation with Mrs. Hansberry, I headed over toward Avery. Oh boy, could

I smell that gum! It wasn't just regular old bubble gum flavor. Or sour apple or peppermint.

It was watermelon.

Exactly like the kind of gum I had stepped on by my seat.

"Where did you get that gum?" I demanded.

Her face paled.

I lifted up the back of my running shoe and ripped off the piece of paper so she could see the wad of green gum stuck to the tread. "Look familiar? You really shouldn't be chewing gum in the theater, Avery."

Leaning forward in her seat, she sneered, "You can't tell me what to do."

"I can. I'm the assistant director."

"That doesn't mean you're Mrs. Hansberry." She shook her head so her braids whipped around. "Just because your mom is principal, you think you can do anything."

"This has nothing to do with my mom, Avery. This has to do with you leaving gum on the floor so I'd step on it. It was meant for me, wasn't it?"

Kids stared at us. I didn't care. I couldn't let Avery get away with this.

"Well, maybe you should be more careful where you walk. You're the assistant director. You're supposed to notice things."

I took a step closer to Avery. "Why are you so mad at me?"

"Don't you remember what we just talked about in your mom's minivan, coming back from that last soccer tournament?"

"Uh, no."

"That figures. You only listen to yourself, Miss Kate the Great! Think you're super special? Well, you're not. I should have been assistant director, not you." She started to list the reasons on her fingers. "I know dance. You don't. I know how to sing. You can't. And I know how to listen."

"At least everyone listens to me when I talk. And I don't sabotage people by crossing out their schedules," I hissed in a voice much louder than I intended. I didn't know it was her for sure, but I figured if I said it, her response might give something away.

"Well, sorry, but you deserved it," she huffed.

Phoenix nodded.

"I can't"—I shook my head so fast the room spun—"I can't believe you think that."

"Quiet," whisper-warned Phoenix, pointing at our teacher. "Mrs. Hansberry." I could see her hurrying toward us.

Avery made a face. "All you want to do is prove you're better than me."

"Not really. I don't even think about you!"

"That's the problem. You don't think about anyone but yourself."

"That's *so* not true!" It wasn't. I thought about Birdie, I thought about the dragons, I thought about—

Mrs. Hansberry now stood next to us. "I don't know what's going on over here, but I'm not pleased." She pursed her lips tightly. "Not pleased at all. You're both at risk of losing your positions in this show if you continue this fight."

"I'm done," said Avery in a sulky voice.

"Me too," I said, and watched Avery stalk away.

If I were a dragon, I would be breathing fire right now.

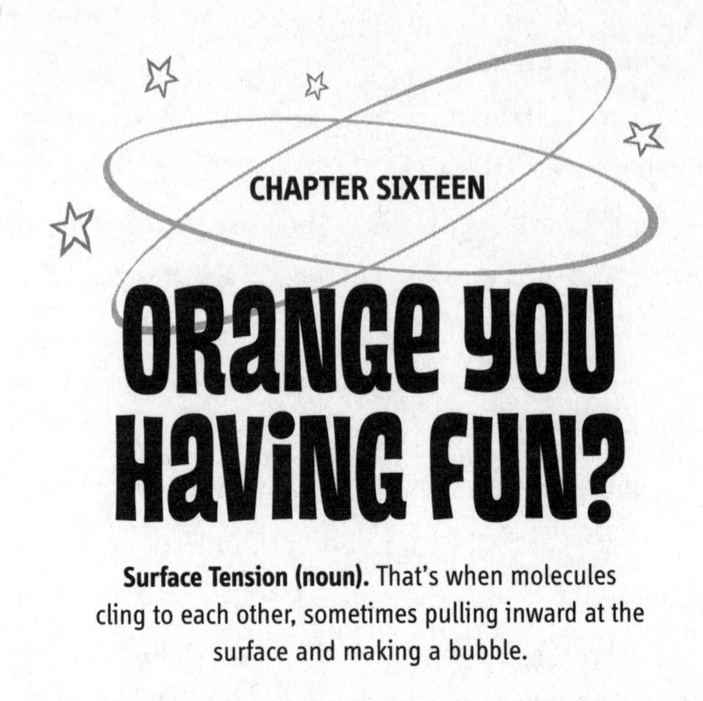

CHAPTER SIXTEEN

ORANGE YOU HAVING FUN?

Surface Tension (noun). That's when molecules cling to each other, sometimes pulling inward at the surface and making a bubble.

THE NEXT MORNING, on Wednesday, despite the blow-up with Avery, I couldn't wait for theater camp to begin. I had on my pink cowboy boots that my grandparents in Texas got me for my last birthday, so I felt more jazzy. But I was mostly jazzed because of a big problem I had to solve. Would my fire breathing plan actually work? The show was Saturday afternoon, only three days away.

It was the tech rehearsal. This meant all of the lighting, the set, and the props had to be in place. It was very

busy. Parents lugged in pieces of scenery, including giant fake boulders, a rainbow banner, and dragon treasure. After everything was set up, Mrs. Hansberry gathered us together in front of the stage.

"Though this isn't a full-dress rehearsal, please put on your costumes so we can make sure everything is working and looks good under the lights." Mrs. Hansberry pointed to a fake volcano and giant tarp painted to look like a cave. "Didn't the crew do a marvelous job with our lovely set?"

A bunch of kids clapped, and I thought about how amazing it was that everything was coming together.

"I want to acknowledge our volunteer parents who dragged in all sorts of props today," continued Mrs. Hansberry. "I'm afraid most of them have left, but we want to offer our heartfelt thanks."

There were more cheers and hoots, and about fifteen minutes later, everyone had on their costumes. The dragons wore bodysuits with their long tails. The unicorns all wore white shirts and their horns. With the house lights down and the spotlight making a large circle of light on center stage, everything did look very different. Almost professional-looking. The volcanos in the set seemed as though they were about to rumble. I thought for a moment about asking if I could make them erupt—Dr. Caroline had a great demo for that—but decided it was more important to focus on the dragons.

Mrs. Hansberry strolled down the aisle and clasped her hands together to greet me. "Kate, I'm quite eager to test out the smoking Cheetos." Like my mom, she seemed to have mind reading abilities. "I'm particularly pleased that Ms. Daly will be joining us this afternoon to help you out."

"Me too!" Mrs. Hansberry told me that Ms. Daly was back from her trip to St. Paul. She said Ms. Daly would take care of the liquid nitrogen if I could take care of the rest.

"I've brought the Cheetos, like I promised," I said.

"Excellent. I knew you would. We'll just roll up our

proverbial sleeves and see what sort of dragon magic we can cook up."

"Awesome!"

"While I tend to some backstage issues," said Mrs. Hansberry, "can you make sure the unicorns go over their dance finale? I'm especially concerned that the lead roles remember all of their cues. It's not easy dancing and remembering lines."

"Sure thing!"

This time I didn't drop my backpack on a seat in the auditorium. This time I kept my backpack with me. On my shoulders. I wasn't going to let anyone mess up my stuff.

But instead of heading backstage, Mrs. Hansberry stepped closer to me and lowered her voice. "Things got a little heated yesterday between you and Avery. I'm hoping things go much smoother today. It's not like you to get into any sort of loud argument. But I know nerves are a little frayed as we get so close to performance time. I appreciate you being calm today."

"No problem," I said, picturing my nerves fraying during the fight yesterday. I didn't think that was scientifically possible, but I'd have to look it up. I really

couldn't wait to try the Cheeto experiment. My stomach was bubbling with excitement. Bubbles meant lots of carbon dioxide trying to escape. It was mostly a happy bubbly feeling but also made me feel like I had too much energy inside.

After lunch, we worked on the second half of the show. Up onstage, the unicorns practiced their finale, and I had the script out with all of the cues marked in red. A cue is the last line before someone new speaks or moves. Actors really need to listen well and say their lines right away, so there's no awkward silence.

Birdie never forgot a cue, and she never forgot any of her lines.

"The dragons are winging overhead. We should hide," said Mia Wong, who played Birdie's sister unicorn.

"If we hide, they will find us," said Steven McFee, a fourth grader, who played their little brother unicorn.

"No hiding!" cried Memito Alvarez, a fifth grader playing the grandfather dragon. "We should fly away."

"But I'm a unicorn and not Pegasus," said Birdie, not even once looking down at her script. Which was amazing. Everyone had to be completely off-book by Friday for the dress rehearsal, but she'd done it two days

early—*and* she had the most lines. Off-book doesn't literally mean off a real book. It just means that the actors need to have memorized all of their lines, and they can't hold a script in their hands. It was another theater thing I learned from Mrs. Hansberry.

I'm really not sure how Birdie memorized everything so quickly. Of course, it was only a twenty-five-minute musical, but still. Mrs. Hansberry said that most plays take weeks and weeks of rehearsal to get off-book. I was proud of everyone for being willing to learn their lines so fast. Especially my BFF.

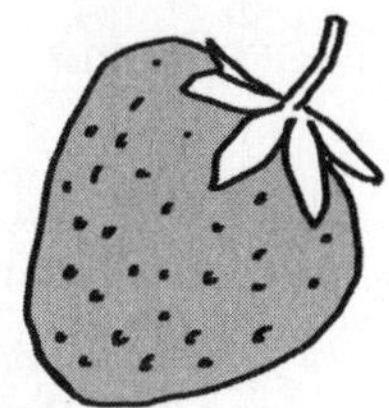

Looking up from the script, I was surprised to see that Birdie's face had turned strawberry red. Was she overheated? Today, for the first time, the spotlight was on, and Elijah and the lighting crew were working on making sure the rest of the lights ran smoothly. No, Birdie couldn't be hot. I rubbed my arms. That didn't make any sense. If anything, it was chilly in the theater.

Instead of keeping her eyes looking straight into the audience during the dance number, Birdie continued to glance at the other performers. With her head turned, Birdie bumped into a fellow unicorn.

"Sorry!" Birdie squeaked.

As they started again doing a little leap, Birdie missed her cue and fell with a clunk.

I rushed toward the stage. "Are you okay?" The other unicorns hovered over her.

"No," said Birdie, her cheeks pink and her eyelashes glistening with tears. "It was my fault. I can't keep count of the dance steps while I'm also remembering my lines."

"Let's take a little five-minute break," I said. "Why doesn't everyone stretch and then run some lines? I'll go over them with Birdie."

Of course, Birdie didn't need to run lines at all. "Birdie, are you all right?" I asked, as we stepped to the back of the theater.

"I don't know what I'm doing up here. Someone else should be in this role. Someone who actually knows how to dance and act at the same time. I'm going to ruin the show."

"Birdie, you can do it! Trust yourself. Stop looking out of the corner of your eye to see what everyone else is up to. I've seen you practice the steps. You've got this!"

Birdie's cheeks turned pink again. One time, I looked up why. Cheeks got pink because of adrenaline,

a hormone. It made your veins open so blood could flow through. It was all part of the flight or fight reaction. Right now, Birdie wanted to run away, and I needed to change all of that.

The best tactic? Get her mind off of her dance number. That's when I told her about the Cheetos demo and how Ms. Daly came back especially to help me.

"I got the really big puffy ones, so they'll hold a lot of liquid nitrogen." I dug into my backpack to pull out the bag. But I couldn't feel them.

Opening my backpack more, I spotted my emergency kit, an extra script, my lunch bag, but no Cheetos! "I'm sure I brought them. I put them right here."

That's when Ms. Daly strode into the theater with a huge grin spread across her face. She had on her blue lab coat and goggles perched on her neck. "The liquid nitrogen is ready to go in the lab," she said. "I can't wait to get started, Kate!"

Getting started would be impossible. Once again, I rummaged through the backpack, checking every pocket. Every nook and cranny. But nothing! What happened to the Cheetos?

CHAPTER SEVENTEEN

A BAD LUCK STREAK

Cohesion (noun). How well a bunch of molecules stick together. It's like when a coach calls for a huddle in soccer. Can the team bunch together and listen? Or is everyone doing their own thing?

EVERYTHING WAS FALLING apart. Avery stood in the back row of the auditorium with Phoenix. I could hear Avery whispering and giggling. She was probably laughing at me. That was enough. I marched right up to Avery. "Thanks a lot for stealing my Cheetos!"

"Your Cheetos? What are you talking about?"

"They were there." I pointed to my backpack. "And now they're gone. Give them back."

"I don't have them!"

On the side of the stage, Mrs. Hansberry stood discussing something with Ms. Daly.

"This isn't funny, Avery. I need them."

"Wow. Someone really needs a snack," said Elijah from the lighting booth.

"The Cheetos aren't for me to eat. They're for the special effects for the dragons." I put out my hand, palm facing up. "Give. Them. To. Me."

Avery stomped her foot. "I already told you, I don't have them."

Phoenix jiggled her charm bracelet. "Avery doesn't even like Cheetos. She wouldn't take them."

"Wouldn't take what?" asked Mrs. Hansberry from the stage. Next to her, Ms. Daly stared at me in surprise.

"Cheetos," said Avery, rolling her eyes. "Kate thinks I took them. Just because she can't find them."

"Well, I don't know where else they could be." I once again rummaged through my backpack. "The bag was in here. I promise." I glanced up apologetically at Ms. Daly, who came in especially to help me out today.

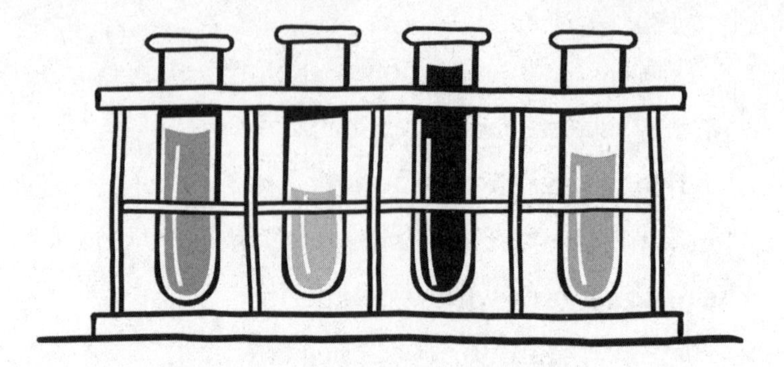

"I'm so sorry," I said, my cheeks heating up. I could practically feel that hormone signaling my veins to open up. My cheeks were probably now phenol red. That's a special dye that chemists use to see if something is an acid or a base. "I don't know what happened." My eyes darted over at Avery. It had to be her.

"I would send someone to the store to buy a bag, but there just isn't enough time," said Mrs. Hansberry. "Well, we have plenty of other things to do."

"I can come back tomorrow," said Ms. Daly.

"Sorry," I mumbled, staring at the floor, which was dusty. That was probably my fault, too. I should have noticed and swept it up so that none of the crew slid while they were working in the dark.

"It's okay," said Ms. Daly.

But it wasn't. I could hear the disappointment in her voice.

“I guess we should get back to work, folks,” said Mrs. Hansberry. The cast headed back onstage.

Only as soon as Birdie whinnied and threw back her mane, her unicorn horn slid off her forehead and toppled onto the floor.

“I’ll re-glue. Don’t worry.” I grabbed a bottle of the stage glue donated by Avery’s dads. Then I squirted a blob on the end of the horn and handed it to Birdie. “There. Just hold it in place.”

“I hope this works,” Birdie wished out loud.

Another groan. This time from Mia. Her horn slid all the way down her forehead. It bumped over the top of her nose, dangling on her chin until she pulled it off.

“Oh. Hold it! I’ll grab more glue for you, Mia.”

Soon the rest of the horns toppled off as well. And no extra amount of glue helped. The horns just got more slippery.

“The glue’s not working,” stated Mia, which was pretty obvious.

“It can’t be dragons vs. horses,” moaned Jeremy.

Mrs. Hansberry strolled closer, frowning thoughtfully. “I’m afraid you’re right—*Dragons vs. Horses* doesn’t quite have the same ring to it.”

Avery wrinkled her nose. "I don't get why this is happening."

"It's probably just not strong enough glue," I said.

"But it's theatrical quality," said Avery with a huff. "My dads use it to stick feathers on masks."

"Masks, did you say?" said Mrs. Hansberry. She inspected the bottle. "Hmm, perhaps this is the wrong sort of glue. Since ours needs to act as an adhesive on skin."

"But not peel anyone's skin off," I said.

"We could tie rubber bands to the horns," suggested Mia. "Or stick them on headbands."

"But these golden horns are perfect," said Birdie. "And the rubber bands or headbands would look so goofy."

"These horns have to work," I said.

Suddenly, the stage went completely dark. "Sorry!" yelled Elijah. "Something's wonky with the lights."

"How are we going to rehearse the dance?" cried Birdie. "With the dragons and unicorns. I mean horses. We can't even see!"

She did have a point.

"Oh my. Children, let's try to remain calm." Mrs.

Hansberry sighed dramatically. "I can see that things are heading in the wrong direction."

"And I didn't even say *good luck*." I clapped my hand over my mouth. "Oh. Sorry! Didn't mean to say that."

Birdie rolled her eyes, and I knew exactly what she was thinking. What bad thing was going to happen next?

CHAPTER EIGHTEEN

Perfectly Rotten

Entropy (noun). The randomness of molecules, like how many different ways they can totally rearrange themselves during a reaction. Sort of like all the different ways a bunch of kids can move their desks to confuse a substitute teacher.

AFTER EVERYONE TOOK A BREAK, loud groans echoed from the lighting booth. Obviously, Elijah and his crew still couldn't figure out how to fix the lights. On the stage, which I'd been lighting with the flashlight from my emergency kit, two unicorns held their horns in place. The others had given up. A half dozen horns lay in a jumbled heap on the floor, like some unicorn horn junkyard.

With a deep sigh, Mrs. Hansberry frowned at her watch. "Elijah, please turn on the house lights." Instantly, the theater was no longer dark, and the magical illusion of Unicornland disappeared. The hulking volcanoes were just giant cardboard rectangles. The rainbow was clearly only a cellophane banner.

"I'm afraid I'm going to end rehearsal a tad early, before anything else breaks," said Mrs. Hansberry. "Everyone is on edge. Why don't you all run around the field for some good fresh air before your parents pick you up?"

A bunch of kids went outside to play a game of pick-up soccer. Normally, I would have joined them, but I needed some space. Even though that only made me feel worse. Settling next to a sugar maple tree with golden and red leaves, I breathed in the cool October air. Sure, it was a bit nippy, but that would help me think more clearly. Underneath my legs, the bumpy knots from the roots of the maple made me feel like I wasn't alone. Actually, I wasn't. Birdie sat silently across from me with her sketch pad balanced on her knees.

"What are you working on?" I asked.

"You'll see." She wiggled her fingers in the air as if she were about to do a card trick.

I opened up my biography about Marie Curie, who won two Nobel Prizes for science. It didn't take me long to get lost in those pages. Wow, Marie Curie was unstoppable. Back when girls couldn't study science in universities in Poland, she met with friends in secret locations that they called a flying university. They moved from building to building, so they wouldn't get caught. I tried to imagine my life if chemistry were off-limits. No more reading science books or watching *Dr. Caroline*. Worst of all, no more experiments.

Whenever I got frustrated, my dad always told me to go outside and blow off some steam. Only sometimes you could be just as frustrated outside as inside. Like Birdie sitting next to me. With a frustrated grunt, she crumpled a sheet from her pad.

"C'mon. It can't be that bad." I reached to pick up the paper, but Birdie grabbed it away.

"Oh, it is. Trust me."

"You working on arms again?"

Birdie hasn't figured out arms yet, so she makes all

of her people with their hands behind their back.

"I'm drawing a unicorn. Mrs. Hansberry asked me to make one for the cover of the program."

"Wow, Birdie. That's awesome. You're great at unicorns."

"I just can't get the proportions right on this one."

"You'll figure it out. I know it."

I could see the hint of a smile. And some of the geese in the sky honked as if they agreed.

Soon I went back inside the theater to check in with Mrs. Hansberry about the plans for tomorrow. Thursday was going to be the rehearsal where everyone was working very hard to be off-book. Mrs. Hansberry also told me that she expected the dress rehearsal to go much better on Friday. But not too much better. "In theater, the rule is if you have a terrible dress rehearsal," she explained in her calm soothing voice, "you'll have a wonderful opening night. And given that our opening night is also our closing night, that's a comforting thought."

As she handed me a checklist of things to do, I tried to relax.

Mrs. Hansberry placed her clipboard in her bag and grabbed her coat. "Expect the dress rehearsal to be a

rather interesting day as we work out the wrinkles. Prepare for Murphy's Law."

"Is that a science thing?"

"Not exactly. More like folk wisdom created by a pessimist. According to Murphy's Law, whatever can go wrong will go wrong."

"Hey, that sounds like entropy. You know, the principle that everything will naturally become a mess."

"They do sound similar, don't they?"

As I started to grab my backpack to leave, Elijah emerged from the lighting booth. "Are things better?" I asked, although I figured with Murphy's Law they shouldn't be.

"With Mr. Anderson's help, yes," he said. Mr. Anderson was a dad volunteering in the booth. "We figured out it was a frayed cord that made the whole thing go kablooey."

"Like our nerves."

"Yeah."

"That's good it's all fixed." Actually, it was bad. I was the assistant director. I shouldn't have left to go outside, even though Mrs. Hansberry had encouraged me to do so. It was my job to make sure everything was okay.

When I grabbed my backpack, I drew in a sharp breath. "Ah! Not again!"

Sticky globs of glue clung to the outside of my zippered compartments. At least this time it was my bag and not my mom's. And I could tell it was the theater glue. That's what I got for sticking horns on unicorns all afternoon.

Later in my mom's minivan on the way home, I thought about all the stuff that went wrong and what I could do tomorrow to make it better. I tapped my chin quickly. Okay, more like frantically.

"What's up, Kate?" asked Mom, who definitely could read minds.

I didn't want to admit that it had been a really tough day. That somehow it felt a little bit like my fault. If I knew what I was doing as assistant director, I could have helped out more.

It was the assistant director's job to keep the show together. To keep things moving as efficiently as an enzyme. Enzymes break down and build molecules snappy quick. And all I was doing was the first part. But I could do better. I knew I could. And I knew I would. First problem to tackle? Unicorn horn glue.

CHAPTER NINETEEN

The Stickiest Situation

Colloids (noun). Mixtures in which the particles are evenly stirred in everywhere; it looks all nice and smooth like milk. Also, like a jump-worthy mud puddle.

FLINGING OPEN THE KITCHEN CUPBOARD, I dug out anything that could be used to make glue. I was determined to figure out a way to keep the unicorn horns from falling off—and to do it quickly, since I really didn't have much time. It was close to dinner. I found a jug of Great Lakes Maple Syrup, wildflower honey, blueberry jam, and a jar of chunky peanut butter.

But I didn't think any of those things would work to make face glue. Though they would all be tasty on bread.

When Dad made a sugar water concoction for the hummingbirds, it got pretty sticky on the counter if it spilled. A sugar mixture could probably be used to stick paper onto someone's forehead, but not a cardboard horn.

On the internet, I discovered that special effects people in Hollywood used something called spirit gum—which sounded perfect for a play full of spirit, which ours was. But it was supposed to be really hard to work with and took forever to dry. Anyway, I didn't have time to order it.

The unicorns needed a strong glue. That way they could whinny, toss their manes, and prance onstage without the horns smashing to the floor.

Adhesive is a more science-y word for glue, and it made me feel like a real scientist to say it. "Adhesive," I said aloud, imagining myself as a professor in a lab surrounded by my future graduate students. "Adhesive. Yes, please pass me some of that adhesive."

Mom popped out of her office in back of the kitchen. "Did you want me, Kate?"

"No, I was just talking to myself," I admitted.

"That's supposed to happen when you're my age,"

said Mom. "When you have too much on your to-do list and get frazzled."

"Guess I'm ten going on forty-one then."

"Thirty-nine," corrected Mom. It was this running joke that she never grew older and that every year was her thirty-ninth birthday. "Anyway, I wanted to let you know that the grant committee just asked for a bit more documentation," she continued. "So back to the grindstone. I'll be in my office if you need me. Tell Dad when you see him that it would be good to eat dinner a little later tonight."

"Sure, I better get back to work, too. I'm trying to make face glue."

"Maybe when you get your formula, you can also glue me to my desk. That way I can stay put and figure out this grant."

"Watch out. I might just try that."

Pacing around the kitchen, I tried to figure out how to make the perfect face glue. Once in Girl Scouts, we had made glue from milk, vinegar, and baking soda. It looked like Elmer's white glue. I decided to try it. I heated a little bit of regular milk from the carton.

When I whisked in the vinegar, the milk curdled.

"That's a chemical reaction," I murmured, staring in fascination at the gloppy pieces that looked like cottage cheese. I used a paper towel to filter out the liquid.

I added a little bit of water and baking soda. The mixture bubbled and looked like sea foam. I knew exactly why. It was the carbon dioxide making a great escape.

The texture was nice and lumpy. If it was too watery, it would slide right off someone's skin. I needed those lumps.

I also needed to find a test subject.

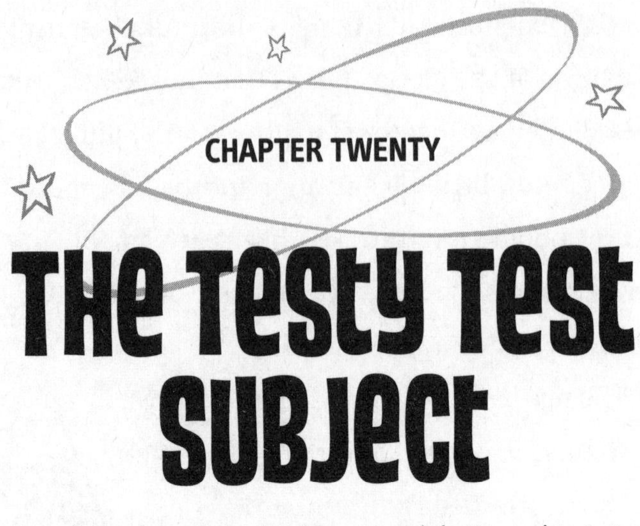

CHAPTER TWENTY

The Testy Test Subject

Experiment (noun). A scientific protocol that's used to test a hypothesis. If you think that chocolate milk tastes better with three scoops of cocoa instead of two, you'll have to test it out.

"LIAM!" I CRIED. "LIAM!" I searched in the family room. Nope. No little brother in sight. Or in the garage. Or outside tossing a basketball in his little kid-sized hoop.

Dribble wagged his tail and brushed up against me. "Where's Liam, Dribble?" I asked, rubbing under his chin. "Probably in his room."

As I bounded upstairs, Dribble trotted after me. The hallway and the bedroom were dark.

"Liam!" I called, flicking on the hall light.

"I'm not here!" called Liam.

I charged into his pitch-black bedroom. The shades were drawn, and there was a Liam-shaped lump under the covers. "What are you doing?"

"Pretending the power went out. Like what happened to you at drama camp. Only I can't use my flashlight to survive."

"Why not?"

"It doesn't have batteries." He let out a whoosh of air. "It's getting really boring in here. There's nothing to see."

"Hey, I've got a great idea. And it's waaaaaay better than a fake power outage."

Five minutes later, Liam sat in a kitchen chair. "Will it hurt?" he asked, pointing at the glue. Then the horn.

"No, it's going to feel cool. As in literally cool and not warm."

He squirmed in his chair.

"Stop moving." The experiment wouldn't work unless he did. But I might as well have told him to stop breathing. "Liam, I mean it."

"I can't." He leaned over and tapped his forehead. "Can't get a song out of my brain."

Grabbing him by the waist, I tipped him upside down. "Now your song will fall right out of your ears," I said.

He giggled and told me it dripped out of his left ear.

I got him right side up again to test out the white glue. With a paintbrush, I coated his forehead with a dab of the glue and plonked on a horn that I had made out of a paper towel roll.

"Okay, now hold it in place," I urged. "At the count of ten, let go. One Mississippi. Two Mississippi—"

"Why do you say Mississippi? We don't live there."

"It's just the state you're supposed to say when you count, Liam."

"That's not fair to the other states. Say Michigan," he insisted.

"Fine." I began to count using Michigan.

Only when I got to six, Liam wiggled so much that the horn slid right off.

"How about you hold it until twenty-five Michigan?" I suggested.

That didn't work either. Neither did one hundred Michigan. Liam said he was as bored as sitting in the dark.

"Maybe you could glue it on Dribble," he said.

"No. He's got fur. I've got to figure out something that will stick to people's skin." The problem had to be that my formula was water-based like Elmer's. Which meant basically any kind of moisture would mess it up. Including five-year-old kid sweat.

"How about use Super Glue," suggested Liam.

"No way. You want me to pull off your skin?"

"Yeah! So I can be a skeleton for Halloween."

I laughed. "Only you would think of that."

Checking online, I finally found a face glue that I could modify.

I gathered:

- 1 1/2 cups water
- 1/2 cup cornstarch
- 1/4 cup corn syrup
- 2 teaspoons white vinegar
- 2 teaspoons food coloring
- 1/2 teaspoon glitter
- 1 medium bowl
- craft sticks

Then I put everything in a saucepan over medium heat. Liam stirred constantly until it was well blended and thick.

"I want to try it!" cried Liam.

"First it has to cool down." I wanted the glue to blend in with the horn, so I added some yellow food coloring and glitter.

This time, we put it on the horn, and Liam held it in place for about a minute. He began to neigh. The horn didn't fall off.

"Toss your head." It still didn't fall off.

"Jump up and down," I instructed. "And toss your head at the same time."

Liam jumped and tossed his head, yelling, "Neigh! Neigh!" Both Mom and Dad poked their heads into the kitchen.

"What are you up to?" asked Dad.

"I'm a unicorn," cried Liam. "And I might be one forever. Because we don't know if the horn will be stuck until I'm old and shriveled like Grandpa Jack."

"That's not nice, Liam," scolded Mom.

"Okay, just old and wrinkled," said Liam.

"You know how to put things very pleasantly."

Dad put his hands up to his face, but I could see he was grinning.

"Let's all pull Liam's horn together," suggested Mom, "and see what happens."

"Maybe my face will come off," said Liam hopefully.

At the count of three Michigan, we pulled the horn right off. Everything was fine, except that my hands were gluey. When I went to open my bag to grab some tissues inside the side zippered compartment, it was filled with glue. Plus, the tissues in the compartment were filled with glue. I couldn't figure out what had happened. I hadn't opened it all day. And there had never been that much glue on my hands.

It was time to do some more investigating.

After swiping inside the compartment with my finger, I inspected it.

Just as I thought.

It was the same bad unicorn glue. Avery's glue. It just had to be Avery. Again.

I thought we were done with this!

CHAPTER TWENTY-ONE

The Real Deal

Matter (noun). Anything that has mass and takes up space. That means kids, dragons, and brownies are matter!

ON FRIDAY MORNING, I paced back and forth in the science lab. My nerves must have been firing extra fast because my skin literally prickled with excitement. Today was the dress rehearsal. This was the very last time to practice before the show on Saturday afternoon.

This was the last chance to figure anything out.

I stood in front of the counter, along with Ms. Daly and the three main dragons, Jeremy, Rory, and Julia. We had tried to test out the dragon breathing special effect

yesterday but we ended up spending so much time getting a couple of dancing and singing numbers right that we didn't have time. Today, we had all arrived at school extra early to test it out.

Soon fog would shoot out of the Cheetos now soaking in the cups of freezing-cold liquid nitrogen on the counter. There was one cup for each dragon.

"Ready for some dragon smoke?" asked Ms. Daly

"Oh yeah!" I said. But it was a teeny lie. We were about to do potentially dangerous special effects. That was, if we didn't follow our protocol with an experienced adult standing next to us.

But we had followed every safety precaution. And Ms. Daly and I knew what we were doing. Just to be safe, we were all wearing the special coated gloves to protect our hands. These were the gloves I had wanted for my birthday. Ms. Daly had convinced the community college to let us borrow them for the play.

She and I guarded the bowls of liquid nitrogen.

"The rules are you must leave the liquid nitrogen in the cup and never touch it," I said.

"Otherwise, it can burn you," finished Ms. Daly. Like me, she wore a lab coat and safety goggles.

Jeremy stepped back. "Are you sure this is safe?"

"Positive. As long as you carefully follow the directions," I said.

The dragons all stabbed a Cheeto with a long wooden spear that looked like an extra-long toothpick.

"Can we eat the Cheetos now?" asked Julia. "I'm hungry."

"Not yet," said Ms. Daly. "Hold your horses. I mean hold your unicorns."

We all laughed at the corny joke.

"We need to wait until *all* the liquid becomes a gas," I said. "Maybe we should all count to ten Michigan to be super safe."

"Ten Michigan?" asked Jeremy, raising his eyebrows.

"It's a thing," I said.

Everyone held their speared Cheeto, waiting. Then after ten Michigans, when the Cheetos released puffs of clouds, I said, "Okay, it's ready!"

The three dragons crunched on their Cheetos and exhaled. Smoke curled out of their nostrils. Okay, not actual smoke. More like fog. I bounced up and down clapping, "It's awesome!"

"The Cheeto tastes pretty good, too," said Jeremy.

"You look like real dragons," Ms. Daly told them.

All of the dragons roared their approval.

"It went so perfectly," I gushed, feeling truly pleased. "Now we just need to see if it will work in the performance. The trick will be to eat your Cheetos behind the curtain and hold your breath while you race onto the stage. It will basically be a one-time stunt as the chorus of other dragons sings, 'Breathe fire, dragons, breathe!' "

Jeremy waved his arm. "This is going to rock!"

Or rather, smoke! I thought.

A few minutes later, we were all back in the theater. I waved at Elijah in the lighting booth. And also at Birdie, who stood with the unicorns as they adjusted their costumes.

Soon, Mrs. Hansberry gathered the rest of the cast

and crew onto the stage. "While this isn't an actual performance with an audience, it's going to be like a real performance," she said. "So we need to treat it like one."

After, we went over a reminder of who needed to be where and when, and Mrs. Hansberry gave a little pep talk. She discussed teamwork and pointed out how well everything was going. "I want to compliment you all for being on time today. Furthermore, I'm pleased to see that everyone is following the rules. Long pants. Closed-toe shoes with sturdy rubber soles."

Before doing this, I didn't know that putting on a musical would be so complicated. Or that you would have to think about safety just like with chemistry.

I knew that Mrs. Hansberry said that a bad dress rehearsal meant a good opening night. But I didn't think I could take too much more Murphy's Law.

I really wanted the dress rehearsal to run smoothly.

And while some actors dropped lines, and I had to give cues, and the lights were behind in a few places, it still felt like a real show.

The unicorn horns finally stayed on everyone's heads. Birdie tossed her mane wildly, and her horn

didn't budge. Without the distraction of the falling horns, Birdie and the rest of the cast were able to concentrate on singing and dancing.

Afterward, we gathered to discuss what we could improve for the actual show tomorrow. Mostly Mrs. Hansberry asked that we go to bed early. Because a good night's sleep was essential for the cast and the crew. And for directors, too. Her eyes met mine.

"I'm truly excited," she said. "I think the audience is going to enjoy this tremendously."

"Yeah, my horn feels like it's part of my head now," said Memito, shaking his mane.

"Thanks to Kate's chemistry skills," said Mrs. Hansberry.

"The dragon smoke looked great from the lighting booth," said Elijah. "I aimed some lights with a blue gel, which made the smoke look smokier."

As everyone was packing away their costumes, I remembered Mrs. Hansberry's warning. "Does that mean we will be in trouble tomorrow," I asked Birdie, "because today went so well?"

"As long as you say *break a leg*, and not those other words." Birdie punched me playfully in the shoulder. "I'm sure everything will be fine. The dragon smoke was seriously cool. I can't believe you figured it out."

I looked at Birdie. "How did you see it?"

"Well." Birdie's cheeks turned pink. "I got here early and peeked in through the classroom window. A few other unicorns did, too. And some of the chorus dragons. It really is awesome."

I was kind of glad I didn't know so many people were watching. It would've made me nervous! But I was happy Birdie got to see how it looked.

"Actually, figuring out the dragon's breath was easy. At least compared to discovering how globs of glue showed up in my backpack yesterday."

That's when I glanced over at Avery, who glanced back at me.

I crossed my arms. "Give me your backpack. I want to look at your bottle of glue."

"Why? It's just glue. Glue is glue is glue."

"Actually, it's not. There are different kinds. And different levels of adhesion. It all depends on if the glue is water based or—"

"I got to go." Avery grabbed her backpack.

"Wait a minute. We need to talk. Why did you put glue on my stuff? You did, didn't you? Twice?"

Avery sighed. "So what if I squirted glue on your bag? Maybe now you'll actually listen to me, Kate."

"What are you talking about? I listen all the time!"

"No. You plow ahead doing whatever you want. You became assistant director when I told you that's what I wanted!"

She had said this the other day, and I really had no idea what she was talking about.

"I'm confused. When did you tell me you wanted to be assistant director?"

"In your mom's minivan. We were coming back from the soccer tournament two weeks ago," Avery said, leaning against the back of one of the audience chairs.

"Well, I didn't hear you," I told her, crossing my arms.

"That's impossible. You were right there." Now her hands were on her hips, and I could see she was getting mad all over again.

I looked around for Birdie. "I seriously don't remember that conversation."

“I was sitting right next to you. Having a conversation with Monica and Heather, who were sitting in the back row.”

“So you weren’t talking to me then,” I said, figuring out when this must’ve happened. “After a game, I just kind of zone out. I’m always super tired from running around.”

“Oh, because you’re never on the bench.”

“I didn’t say that.” I rolled my eyes. “Avery, you were only on the bench during the second half. I’m hardly on the bench because we don’t have any backup defenders.”

Walking over, Birdie waved her arms. “Stop. There’s no point arguing about any of this. Does it matter right now?”

“Not really,” I admitted.

“And it’s true, Kate,” said Birdie “You’re my best friend and I love, love, love you. But sometimes, you do get stuck in your own head and don’t pay attention to what’s going on around you.”

“Well, I—Okay. Yeah.” I stared at my shoes. “Next time, tell me directly.”

“Next time,” said Avery, “try to listen more.”

I breathed in. My parents tell me to do this when I get worked up. "I didn't mean to—you know, not listen. I'm sorry about that."

Avery bit her lip. "Well, I could have said it to you directly, I guess. My dads get on me all of the time about that. I wanted to impress them so they'd give me more responsibility around their theater, and I thought being assistant director would be a good first step. That's why I wanted it so badly."

I sighed. I knew what it was like to want to impress your parents and show them that you were responsible. "You're an amazing dance captain, though—and assistant choreographer. The dragons never would've been as great as they are if you weren't there to show them the steps."

"Thanks. And you're really organized. You came up with some really great science things that made our show cooler. So I guess it all worked out after all. I'm sorry I was a jerk about it."

"And I'm sorry I wasn't paying attention to you in the car," I said.

It felt good to have apologized and to hear Avery apologize, too. But there was still one mystery left unsolved.

"So where did you put my Cheetos the other day?" I asked. "Did you eat all of them?"

"I promise that one wasn't me." Avery crossed her heart. "Look. I'm super sorry about the glue. And messing with the schedule. But I didn't eat a single Cheeto."

"Okay, I believe you," I said.

But I still had no idea who took my Cheetos.

CHAPTER TWENTY-TWO

N-R-G!

Kinetic Energy (noun). A solid has a low amount of kinetic energy. A liquid has more kinetic energy. Like when the DJ has kicked up the bass. The liquid molecules are moving and having a dance party.

IT WAS SATURDAY AFTERNOON, October 17, and our show was actually about to happen! Mentally, I went through the list of everything we needed. The stagehands and the props were in place. The actors waited backstage.

Right now, it felt as if a dozen balls bounced in my stomach.

The call time had been 12:30 p.m. (the time when the cast and the crew needed to arrive). At 2:00 p.m., the

curtain would rise, and the show would officially begin.

By 1:30 p.m. everyone was in costume and makeup. The house lights were up but not for much longer. Elijah and his crew had already performed their lighting check to make sure the equipment worked.

I had gone through a prop checklist with the backstage crew.

The scenery had been repositioned perfectly into place.

The scripts were jammed in backpacks. Everyone today was really, *really* off-book.

As the assistant director, I had to react quickly. But not panic.

Still, I couldn't stop worrying.

I waved at Elijah and the crew running the lighting board.

"Everyone, please gather on the stage," said Mrs. Hansberry. Soon, a couple dozen kids grouped around us. "Whatever you do, keep plowing ahead," she added. "If you need to, ad-lib until you get back on track."

"Yes," I said. "And I've got the script right here. I'll whisper a line if you forget. And if that doesn't work, I'll shout. And if that doesn't work, I'll march onstage."

"Fantastic," said Mrs. Hansberry. "We have plan B, C, and D."

I glanced down at the prompt book with all the cues and technical notes for the show. Today, I shouldn't have to call out any cues, but I knew exactly what I needed to do if I had to.

"It's time to get in a circle," said Mrs. Hansberry. "This is a time-honored theater tradition."

The cast and crew made a big circle on the stage. "This, my friends, is a very special circle. I would like for you all to say the letters *N-R-G*."

"N-R-G," we said.

"Louder," said Mrs. Hansberry.

"N-R-G," we said.

"Now repeat it. Louder and faster." We did until everyone broke into giggles as we realized we were all saying *energy*.

"We are going to give energy," continued Mrs. Hansberry. "Lots of it. Crew and cast alike. Now let's gather tighter." With our right arms crossed over our left arms, Mrs. Hansberry had us hold hands with people on either side. I was holding hands with Birdie on my right and Phoenix on my left.

"We work as an ensemble to make a helping hand," said Mrs. Hansberry. "And we need all of our fingers. Each of you contributes and together we are one group. There are no small parts. No small roles. It takes all of us coming together for this one-act musical to work."

Then she had us close our eyes and she gave energy to the person on the left by squeezing their hand and the energy was passed around from person to person. Nobody said a word.

When everyone had finished, Mrs. Hansberry said, "Break a leg, everyone." Then she had the cast and crew turn out of the circle by uncrossing their arms.

"Curtain time is in twenty minutes. Prepare to turn down the house lights at my command. I'm opening up the doors. The audience will now be seated."

We scrambled into place as the sound of theatergoers filled the once empty theater. Somewhere in the audience sat my parents and Liam. I was too afraid to peek.

If I listened really hard, I thought I could hear Liam's raspy little voice.

The cast and crew held their breath as we waited for the show to begin.

And then the house lights went down.

The curtain opened.

Showtime!

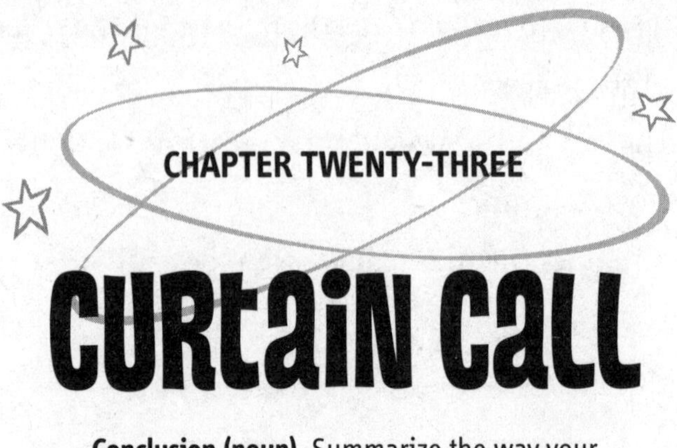

CHAPTER TWENTY-THREE

CURTAIN CALL

Conclusion (noun). Summarize the way your results support or contradict your original hypothesis. Like anytime you say, "Told you I was right!"

UNBELIEVABLY, INCREDIBLY, the show went really well. Sure, there were a couple of slip-ups. One of the dragon's tails came off. And a unicorn mane slipped sideways. And one of the doors wouldn't open to a dragon's cave.

But the energy (or N-R-G) was great. Birdie remembered all of her dance steps and didn't look at the other unicorns. Elijah's lightning storm special effects were awesome. During the finale, the lead dragons breathed smoke out of their noses. The crowd went wild.

My mom stood up in the first row. And my dad,

Ms. Daly, and Liam. And the rest of the audience. The clapping was thunderous. There were whistles and cheers.

As the cast took their bows, Mrs. Hansberry nudged me on the shoulder. “Go out onstage, Kate.”

“Are you sure?”

“Very.” Mrs. Hansberry pushed me forward with the rest of the cast to take our final bow. Elijah flashed the spotlight right on me, which made me blink, but I couldn’t help grinning. I’m sure everyone could see my tonsils.

Then Avery stepped out of the line of actors and toward the front of the stage. For a moment, I held my breath. What was she up to?

My stomach plummeted.

“There’s a tradition in my dads’ theater of acknowledging the director with a bouquet of white roses,” said Avery. A stagehand hurried onstage and handed her the bouquet. “Mrs. Hansberry, could you please come onstage?”

Mrs. Hansberry strolled onstage, with her clipboard

still in her hand, and accepted the flowers. "We also have flowers for our accompanist, Mrs. Hagel." Avery pointed to Mrs. Hagel, who waved from her upright piano. Then another stagehand scurried out and handed her a bouquet of yellow tulips.

"And also for our assistant director," said Avery, waving a bunch of Texas bluebonnets.

I was shocked. I bowed again and accepted the bouquet. "Thanks!" My parents and Liam beamed. "And thank you for being the greatest cast and crew. The show was amazing!"

"Yes, you children were wonderful," said Mrs. Hansberry, gesturing at the crew with a sweep of her long arm. "We're ever so thankful for all of our volunteers who helped with makeup, costumes, and set building. And parents, thank you for your patience. I know that many nights during our fall break were spent running lines at home and finding props. Thank you for lending me your marvelous children. Good night!" She threw out a kiss. And then Elijah made the lights blink as if we were at a disco. There was a burst of thundering applause until the house lights went back on.

The show was over.

Parents flooded the stage. Suddenly, everyone was taking photos and giving hugs.

Liam brought me a silver Mylar balloon that said STAR SISTER.

"Thanks," I said.

"It was really good," said Liam, waving the program with Birdie's awesome unicorn on it.

"It was fantastic," said Mom. "I can't believe how much you all accomplished in a week."

"The dragon smoke was so cool." Liam tilted his head. "Was it real?"

"Yes, Liam. Those were real dragons."

Liam threw back his head and laughed. "Ha-ha. You're kidding. Those were Cheetos. I could smell them."

"I'm proud of Kate for figuring out those smoking Cheetos," said Dad. "It was quite the complex operation." Dad put his hand on my shoulder. "So, gang, ready for some ice cream?"

"Yes!" cheered Liam.

I scurried away to find Birdie and Elijah and let them know it was ice cream time. It didn't take a lot of convincing. We all jumped up and down singing. "I scream, you scream. We all scream for ice cream!"

Out of the corner of my eye I could see Avery looking at us longingly.

I raced over to her. "Want to come to McSweeny's with us?"

Avery looked up at her dads. "Can I?"

"Absolutely, sweetie," said her dad Mark, who nudged her dad Andrew.

"Better get yourself a double scoop," said Andrew as he handed Avery a twenty-dollar bill. "We expect change."

We all left the theater together.

We had our own kids' table at McSweeny's. My parents sat in the front of the ice cream parlor on their own little date. I got my cone with a double scoop of salted caramel dipped in chocolate sprinkles, my favorite.

"Want to try mine?" asked Liam. "It's bubble-gum flavor."

I shook my head. "No, thanks, I'm good." I eyed my little brother suspiciously. "It's not like you to share."

"I'm so happy!" he cried. "The dragons used magic Cheetos! You know, a whole bag of them appeared in your backpack one morning, just waiting for me to eat them!"

I cupped my hand over my mouth. "Oh my goodness. You ate them before I brought them to school." The mystery of the missing Cheetos was finally solved.

Liam nodded and licked his drippy cone.

"Told you it wasn't me," Avery said, laughing.

Elijah waved his finger. "I'm keeping an eye on you, Liam."

"Especially with anything involving orange snack food," said Birdie.

"Next time, just ask first, Liam. Okay? But I can't blame you. Those were definitely yummy magic snacks." Then I winked at my friends.

At that moment, I realized something big. Friends, just like polymers, must stick together. They should listen to each other, too. And while science club would always be my favorite thing to do, drama wasn't so bad either. Especially when chemistry was involved.

UNICORN GLUE

MATERIALS

- ☆ 1½ cup water
- ☆ ½ cup cornstarch
- ☆ ¼ cup corn syrup
- ☆ 2 teaspoons white vinegar
- ☆ 2 teaspoons food coloring
- ☆ ½ teaspoon glitter
- ☆ 1 unicorn horn
- ☆ 1 medium bowl
- ☆ 1 medium saucepan
- ☆ Craft sticks
- ☆ Hot plate or stove top
- ☆ 1 spoon

TO MAKE YOUR UNICORN HORN

1. Get a piece of paper.
2. Draw a large triangle with a rounded bottom on the paper.
3. Cut it out.
4. Roll the paper into a cone and tape or glue it together.
5. Decorate your unicorn horn.

PROTOCOL

1. Add all ingredients (except the unicorn horn, bowl, craft sticks, and spoon!) to a medium saucepan.
2. Heat the mixture over medium-low heat for approximately 7 minutes, stirring continuously.
   NOTE: Depending on your heat settings, it may take up to 20 minutes. Be patient!
3. The mixture will thicken into a frosting-like substance. This is the glue.
4. Take the saucepan off the heat and allow the glue to cool for 5 minutes.
5. Transfer the glue to a medium bowl.
6. Use craft sticks to spread your glue!

HOW IT WORKS:

Glue is extra sticky because it has both adhesive and cohesive forces. When we combine these two properties, we are able to glue anything we want together. Let's think about an easy example, like gluing a poster of the periodic table to the wall. When a molecule (formed when two or more atoms join together) likes to make bonds with other molecules, we say it has strong adhesive forces. The best glues have extremely strong adhesive forces because they have to stick to both the poster and the wall.

The cohesive forces allow the glue to stick to itself—just like peanut butter stays together in a clump. When a molecule likes to make a bond with itself, it has strong cohesive forces. A perfect glue sample has great adhesive and cohesive forces so that the poster is stuck to the glue and the glue is stuck to the wall (adhesive-cohesive-adhesive).

It's important to give the glue time to dry before testing its strength. As the molecules from the atmosphere interact with the glue, the water evaporates from the glue mixture. This process forces the glue to harden, activating the "glue" properties we love. The resulting hard glue layer is extremely strong and very difficult to break. The strength of the glue is determined by what it's made of and what it can stick to.

DR. KATE BIBERDORF, also known as Kate the Chemist by her fans, is a science professor at UT–Austin by day and a science superhero by night (well, she does that by day, too). Kate travels the country building a STEM army of kids who love science as much as she does. You can often find her breathing fire or making slime—always in her lab coat and goggles.

You can visit Kate
on Instagram and Facebook @KatetheChemist,
on Twitter @K8theChemist,
and online at KatetheChemist.com